THE WINTER PRINCE

CONSTANCE LOPEZ

D1714768

To Momma: Thanks for letting me steal books off your shelves for years, and for letting me talk your ear off about any and everything book-related, even when you were trying to sleep.

To Daddy: Thanks for reading *The Hobbit* and *Lord of the Rings* to me as a kid. And thanks for encouraging my love of superheroes with all our movie dates.

Both of you fostered my love of stories, of fantasy, and of writing.
I love y'all.

CONTENTS

THE CURSE

O nce upon a time, a great threat swept over the Winter Court of the Elyri, and in his desperation, the Winter Prince, most beautiful and terrible of his kind, sought allies far and wide.

Far to the south, the Summer Queen agreed to send aid if only the Winter Prince would marry her daughter. The fateful bargain was struck.

When the final attack came, Winter, along with their Summer allies, fought long and hard—and no one harder than the Winter Prince himself—until all their foes were slain. But the prince, heady with battle-glory and self-righteous pride, rashly forswore the Summer Court, claiming their aid had done less than nothing against the tide of enemies.

And so the bargain was broken, and, as was her right, the Summer Queen cursed the northern Elyri:

Summer shall rule in Winter's land
While beast confines the heart of man
Until the strongest of the weak
A lifelong devotion does speak
And restores a Heart of Winter

CHAPTER I
REVI

B lood coated Revi's paws and muzzle. Annoyance prickled across his hide, making his fur stand on end. He hated to be dirty, to let the gore and grime cling to him after a battle. He wanted nothing more than to return home, wash the death from himself, and curl up on the hearth.

But as he got closer to the castle, he felt a foreign presence. Intruders. They didn't have the hot stickiness to them that the monstrous *zruyeds* did, but they were still *other*—their signatures did not carry the familiar cold wildness of a Winter Elyri. They didn't belong in his Court.

Growling in irritation, Revi slipped through the forest, his dappled silver and white coat mingling with the play of light and shadows between the trees.

He hadn't made it much farther when a sense of loss scraped sharply along his magical awareness, like a set of claws against his mind. Something was horribly wrong.

He pressed his magical awareness out as he neared his castle. Intruders indeed. He could sense at least a dozen of them. He pushed himself faster. He would rid himself of them just as he had rid the Court of the widened as Revi spoke, but Revi continued, ignoring the play of emotions across the man's face, "You will give her that rose, and she will return by the next full moon, or I will come and hunt down every last one of you."

Silence descended on the garden as full and still as a midwinter night.

"Then what will you do with her?" the leader asked. He stood tall, kept his voice steady, but he could not hide the fear in his scent. It made Revi's predator instincts sharpen. "I won't offer a woman for you to murder in our place."

"She will be unharmed. She must only stay for a year and a day, according to Elyri custom, and during that time, she will be cared for, given anything she asks, protected like one of our own." The man's expression still held disbelief, so Revi growled and added, "So I swear it on my name as the Heart of the Winter Court." Magic threaded out of him as he crafted the bargain—thinner than if he had used his true name, but he wouldn't give that to humans, not even for this. A nameless bargain would have to suffice.

The man's eyes widened yet again; perhaps he too felt the magic as it wound around Revi and him and the rose in his hand, anchoring there.

"And it's that or my prince will ensure that none of you leave—ever," Enlo added, his voice pleasant and entirely at odds with his words.

The humans behind the leader shifted, sharing glances, adjusting their grips on their swords as if they actually thought those would do anything against Revi.

Revi bared his fangs. He hoped the man would opt to fight. He'd rather fresh blood on his claws than the care of a human woman.

7

The man drooped and sighed heavily. "It'll be as you say. I will escort her back here myself—or I will return alone and offer myself up to die."

Maybe the humans had no great beauties to offer. Maybe the man still doubted Revi's word. He chose to ignore that possibility before it tempted him to kill the man here and now to be done with it.

"Escort her back," he said, "but do not enter my castle grounds again. Humans, save for her, are not welcome here."

The man's jaw clenched, but Revi turned toward the castle. He took a few steps and then paused and looked back over his shoulder. "And if any of you touch my frostroses again, I will know, and you will have lost your last chance at freedom. Now get out of my Court."

With that, he left, his hide still prickling with anger.

Enlo had gotten what he wanted; a human woman was coming to the Winter Court.

Revi only hoped this bargain did not fail as spectacularly as the last one he'd made had.

CHAPTER 2
KIENNA

W hen the sounds of horses and calls of men filtered up to Kienna through her window, she dropped the embroidery she was working on and ran to look out.

Papa. A grin spread across her face. She pushed off the windowsill and dashed from her room and down the hall. He'd been gone for weeks, a little piece of her soul missing. She skirted the servant bringing in his saddlebags up the main staircase, crossed the front hall, and hurried across the courtyard.

"Papa!" she cried, her joy bursting from her, too much to be contained until she could wrap her arms around him.

At the sound of her voice, he looked up, but instead of his slow, steady smile, his expression was full of... pain. Grief.

He shuttered it quickly, dropping a stoic mask that was far more in character for him over his features.

Kienna's steps slowed, her heart dropping. She hadn't seen such behavior from him since Mama's death. Had he lost someone on his mission? She scanned him for injuries, but while he looked travel weary, he didn't look like he'd sustained any life-threatening injuries of his own. But any manner of accidents could happen on a patrolling mission into the mountains beyond Makaria. She swallowed her worry and closed the gap between them, clasping his hands in her own, giving him a warm smile.

"Welcome home, Papa."

His hand squeezed around hers, and he drew her into a hug, crushing her to his chest. "I missed you, my flower." There was an odd catch to his voice, almost as if he was fighting back emotion. Fighting back tears.

Kienna pulled away and searched his face. "Papa, what's wrong? What happened on your patrol?"

He tensed, giving her a smile that was entirely built of lies. "Nothing, my flower. All's well."

"No, it's not." She was entirely certain it was *not* all well. A sick feeling twisted up in her, a mimic of how she'd felt when the news of Mama had first reached them years before. But Papa stood before her, whole and hale. He wasn't lost on the road like Mama had been. So why did she feel like she was about to lose him the way they'd lost Mama? The discordance of it stabbed into her. "Please, Papa. Don't lie to me. Whatever this is, don't try to bear it alone."

Her plea broke through his resistance, and with it, his mask crumbled away, leaving his grief on full display in the lines of his face. "Oh, my flower, I'm so, so sorry."

Her fingers tightened on his arms. "What are you sorry for?" Whatever she'd expected him to say, that wasn't it.

"You asked me for the most interesting flower I could find while on my patrol."

"Yes?" She glanced around, unsure why he would bring that up. "How could a flower cause such grief?"

He choked back a humorless laugh. "I found you the rarest flower imaginable, and it cost a life."

She jerked back, eyes widening. "What... Did you lose someone on your journey?" Her gaze slipped over him again. "Are you hurt? Are you poisoned?" Maybe she'd just missed the signs.

He squeezed his eyes shut against her barrage of questions. "Let me finish, my flower." He turned and reached into the saddlebag on his horse, the last one the servants hadn't taken yet. He withdrew a rose, and it was unlike any she had ever seen.

It was the size of man's fist, which was twice that of any of the roses that ever grew in her own garden, and it looked untouched, as pristine as if it had just been plucked from a bush, not pulled from a saddlebag after days of travel. But instead of being red, or pink, or even a normal white rose, it was a brilliant sheen of silver that shimmered, looking at turns blindingly white and blue and even as clear as crystal when it turned in the light. Her breath caught in her throat, and she reached trembling fingers out to it.

At her movement, her father's fingers tightened on the stem. She looked up at him. "Where did you get this?"

"We stumbled on some elven-like people in the mountains," he said, his voice tight. "The Elyri. The Lorili elves call them fae. At first I thought it was an abandoned castle, and when I saw this rose, I thought of you and I picked it, but as soon as I did, a man appeared... and then a horrible beast—a frostcat larger than I've ever seen before. The beast claimed we'd invaded his Court. He demanded either my life or the lives of my men."

Kienna flinched. She gripped his hand. "But you're here. And so are your men." She gestured at his soldiers unloading behind him. "How did you get away? Did you slay the beast?"

"No." He avoided her gaze. "No, I've only come to say goodbye."

Her heart was crushing. This was a horrible, awful nightmare. "That makes no sense. Why would he let you leave if you're just to return and die? There has to be another way."

Something flickered across his expression, igniting hope in Kienna's chest. "There *is*. Tell me, Papa."

Agony twisted Papa's face. His eyes glistened with unshed tears. The sight caught Kienna's breath. She had only seen Papa cry once, right after Mama's disappearance—when they first learned she had died, that there was no finding her and saving her.

"Let me help," she whispered.

He shook his head. "It doesn't matter. I won't take that path. I won't offer you or any other—" He cut himself off abruptly and swore before shooting a dark glare at her. "It doesn't matter."

But he couldn't take back his slip. Kienna latched onto it like her only anchor in a flood. "Offer me how? Other what?"

He tugged his hand from hers and started pacing, his grip flexing on his sword hilt. "No."

"Papa." The word was half-plea, half-steel. She *needed* to know what he refused to say.

"His third option, the only one where no one need die—or so he claimed"—he scoffed, making it clear how much he trusted such a claim—"he asked for a woman, unmarried and beautiful. He promised she'd be unharmed, so long as she stayed for a year and a day."

Kienna swallowed a breath, and then another; it felt like she wasn't getting enough air.

He continued, "I contacted Cuimal, spoke with the elven ambassador and the mages there. The elves know of the fae. They're distant cousins, apparently, sequestered in the mountains, but their relationship with their magic has... changed over the years. The elves claim the fae cannot speak a lie, but they deal in bargains and revel in deception nonetheless. And once a bargain is made with a fae, you must meet the conditions, or you suffer an even worse fate." He looked away, his voice gravelly. "I only returned to say goodbye. I won't send you to your death for my own folly, you or any other young woman. But I didn't want to go to mine without seeing you one last time."

Her heartbeat rang in her ears. "What?" she whispered. "Papa, no. You said yourself if I go, they won't harm me." Her thoughts rolled from her lips before she'd even fully formed them, had a chance to reflect on them, but she meant every word. It wasn't even a question. "I will give a year of my life so you can have the rest of yours."

He swiveled on her. "Did you hear nothing I said? They're deceivers, all of them."

"You just said they can't lie outright."

He shook his head violently. "How do we know the elves are right and they can't lie? And even if that's true, how do they define protection? There is *no* guarantee that any woman who goes to their Court will ever come out."

Kienna shivered as the truth of that sank into her, but her resolve only settled tighter on her shoulders. "Perhaps. But maybe the elves speak true and the bargain is legitimate. Please, Papa. I've already lost Mama."

"As have I." He stepped in, brushing the tear streaking down her cheek away. "And you want me to risk losing you too?"

"That's the thing, Papa. If I go, I might return. There's a risk that I won't, yes, but not a certainty. But if you go, you'll—" Her voice broke. She had to gather herself before she could continue. "You going would be a certainty. And it's a certainty I can't live with. Let me do this."

"I cannot ask that of you, Kienna. I would not."

"You're not asking," she said softly. "I'm telling you: I will not let you waste your life foolishly."

His eyes begged her, pulling at her heart in ways even his words could not. "I cannot send you alone into a beast's den."

"My mind is made up. I'm going." She drew in a tremulous breath and set her jaw. "I am going," she repeated, meeting his eyes and letting her determination shine through.

He searched her gaze and brushed rough, calloused thumbs along her cheeks. "I'm so sorry, Kienna."

"I was the one who asked for a stupid flower." She tried but failed to manage a simple smile. "I will live with the consequences of my actions, and I will come back to you."

His eyes slid shut again and he nodded, though it looked like it broke his heart to do so. "Then we leave at dawn if we are to return in time to meet the beast's deadline."

CHAPTER 3
ENLO

E nlo found Revi in the library. Today, his cousin was a giant winter wolf, fur an ombre ripple of silver and white. He lay on the largest sofa, a wide book of the Court's reports spread before him. No matter how Enlo was used to seeing Revi in beast form, there were some things he would never grow accustomed to—like seeing an animal reading a book with the sort of intensity and focus he attributed to Revi in years past.

The wolf didn't look up at him as he used his nose to turn the page. Enlo sauntered across the room and settled into the arm chair nearest to Revi. His cousin read, and Enlo stared at him until Revi emitted a low rumble and fixed his gaze on Enlo.

"Did you have something to tell me, or did you just come to ogle?"

"You know," Enlo said conversationally, leaning back and throwing one arm over the side of the chair, "I'm certain a talking, literate beast would make quite the spectacle in the human lands."

Revi growled again. Enlo chuckled, but he quickly sobered, his mind too preoccupied to keep the levity going.

"I haven't had a chance to look over those yet." He gestured to the papers before Revi. "What news?"

Revi scanned the page. "The Master of the Hunt reports fewer prey in the northern forest."

Enlo grimaced. "So soon?"

Revi grunted his affirmative.

"That's..."

"Bad."

"Yes." Enlo tapped a finger on his knee. "What of the western slopes?"

Revi shook his head. "No better."

Enlo swallowed. Despite the regular rain—for they still got a decent amount—the Winter Court was bleeding out. The animals could feel the land's decay and were leaving on their own.

Enlo hesitated. After being cursed by the Summer Queen, Revi hated any mention of any of the other Courts, but... "Any luck changing the trade agreements with the other Courts? Have any of them agreed to send more food stores?"

Revi's lips curled back in a silent snarl. "No."

Enlo hadn't expected any luck there either—the other Courts could only spare so much of their own crops—but the question had needed to be asked.

"I did hear from the steward," Enlo said quickly; better to draw Revi's attention from the other Courts before he was too riled to discuss anything else. "The farmers' latest crop of summer squash did somewhat better. Half of it yielded produce instead of a third."

Revi's side-eye made it clear he saw through Enlo's attempt at cheer on the topic. "And his other crops?"

Enlo shifted. "The same as before." Which was very poorly. Even the summer crops refused to grow, thanks to the curse.

Revi's silence tightened with his tension. When he spoke, his voice was low and broken. "My Court is dying."

Enlo was out of his seat in an instant. He dropped to his knee beside Revi's sofa. He dug a hand into his cousin's shoulder, gripping the thick, soft fur there. "No. No, we won't let it. There's still the caves. Our scouts are exploring them, and their reports are promising. We can develop them into new homes for our people—"

"And how long will that take? And how long will that sanctuary last without a reliable food source?" Revi tilted his head away from Enlo, hiding his gaze. "The Winter Court is dying, Enlo. We can't stop it. Eventually the land will wither away entirely."

Enlo sat back on his heels. "We can slow it, though. Slow it until you win the human's heart, and then the curse will break and the Court will be restored."

Revi huffed, the sound too quiet for Enlo to discern Revi's feelings from it.

"Is everything ready for her?" Enlo asked.

Revi's muscles tightened under Enlo's hand. "What is there to prepare? The rooms are clean. There's food in the kitchens."

Enlo frowned. It would be impossible to miss how reluctant Revi was about their impending guest, but Enlo wished he would try a little harder. The fate of the Winter Court depended on Revi getting this stranger to fall in love with him, and no one was going to fall in love with a surly beast.

"Are *you* ready?" Enlo tried again.

"There's nothing to prepare," Revi growled, baring deadly sharp fangs. "I will be here. She will be here. What more do you want, Enlo?"

"Something other than anger would be nice. A sign that you care."

Revi's claws dug into the cushion beneath him. "I care. You know I do."

"I know you do." Enlo leaned forward and let some of his frustration leak into his voice. He needed Revi to hear this. He needed Revi to set aside his pride for once. If Enlo were in his place... but he wasn't. Revi was the prince of the Winter Court. Revi was the one who mattered, and all Enlo could do was try to get him to care like Enlo did.

"Give this girl a chance, Revi. Yes, she's human, but there are legends of Elyri-human matches. They're not mindless beasts."

"No, that designation falls to me," Revi agreed darkly. "Humans are just weak."

Enlo rolled his eyes. "Of course they are. They hold nothing of power—they don't have our beauty, their magic is sporadic, and their physical attributes are as weak as a child's. But you don't need her to be powerful. You need her affection. Just enough to say that vow and free us from this cursed summer."

"I have already told you I will try, cousin." There was an edge to Revi's tone. Not anger, but rather pain of some sort.

Enlo sat back. That was probably the best he was going to get at the moment. "Just remember your promise."

"How could I forget with a buzzing little fly in my ear?" Revi's tail flicked back and forth.

Enlo grinned. "Someone has to buzz in your ear. All the other Elyri are too afraid to. I consider it my sacred duty."

Revi barked a short laugh. "How many days left?" he asked after a lull.

"A week."

The past few weeks had passed at a crawl slower than moss grew, an insistent itch at Enlo's shoulders as he waited for this mysterious woman to arrive.

He had taken to haunting the library himself, poring over the scroll enshrined at the end, under the great window that overlooked Revi's frostrose bush. Now more than ever, it seemed vital to understand every nuance of the Summer Queen's curse. If Revi failed to secure the affection of this human, it was a very real possibility that their Court wouldn't survive long enough for him to get a second chance.

Enlo pulled his gaze away from the scroll under the window. "I've already sent out orders to all the denizens of the Winter Court to let her party—if she is not alone—pass unharmed."

"Your foresight, as always, cousin, is far better than mine." Revi stretched and hopped from the sofa, brushing past Enlo. He nosed the book shut and sat back on his haunches. "Should we assign a maidservant to her?"

Enlo rose and settled on the sofa Revi had just vacated, withholding the smile that nearly sprang to his face. The question showed Revi was at least giving *some* consideration to the coming guest, despite his gruff words, and that gave Enlo hope.

"I'll find someone, if you so wish."

Revi's head tilted as he considered. "Yes," he finally said. "Yes, that's wise. Our people may not know anything about caring for humans, but, at the very least, another woman will understand any feminine needs that arise."

"I'll have someone picked out by the end of the day."

Revi shifted, pushing off his haunches and shuffling his front paws a bit. After a moment, he rested his large head on Enlo's knee and closed his eyes. It was a rare moment of affection from his cousin, something Enlo had never seen him do with anyone else and only occasionally with Enlo himself.

Enlo released a sigh and slowly brought his hand to rest on Revi's head. "I have faith in you, Revi. I know you can save us all."

"With the help of a *human*," Revi muttered. He gave a sigh of his own and turned his head away ever so slightly from Enlo. "You have always had far more faith in me than I deserve, cousin."

"I have always had exactly the right amount of faith in you, my prince." He let his hands curl into Revi's fur. "Have you tried dreamwalking to see if they're near?"

"I can't walk her dreams when I have not even met her yet," Revi said, his voice low and rumbly.

"The leader," Enlo pointed out. "He said he would journey back with her. Have you searched for him?"

A huff escaped Revi. "No," he admitted. "I haven't. But if no one arrives by the end of the week, I most certainly will."

Enlo grimaced. "Let's hope it doesn't come to that."

Revi gave a low huff of noncommittal agreement.

"You know," Enlo said after several minutes of silence. "If you can figure out what her favorite animal is and shift into that form, that would probably make your task that much easier."

Revi slit one eye open to glare at Enlo. "I thought the goal was to get her to marry me, not adopt me as a pet."

Enlo grinned. "Of course it is, but a pet is a good start. Just look at how well you're fulfilling my dreams of having a loyal hound right now." He gave an overexaggerated scratch behind Revi's ears to emphasize his point.

Revi growled. "Do that again and I will show you exactly what sort of pet I can be."

Enlo bit back a chuckle. "You protest, but you can't say that you don't enjoy it." Revi growled again, this time lower, and Enlo laughed. "See?"

"Enlo," Revi said. "Shut up."

CHAPTER 4
REVI

A few days passed restlessly for Revi, and his agitation only heightened when a scout came at dawn warning humans would reach the castle by midday. He had no appetite, and irritation scraped under his hide at every little thing, so he sent away the meat the chef had prepared for him and took to his garden. He shifted to his frostcat form and climbed a nearby tree, glaring at his frostroses and hoping Enlo wouldn't come to find him.

It was a few hours after dawn when the wind blew their scent to him like a smack on his nose. It was one part familiar—that irritating mix of steel and oil and leather from the leader of the group—but entwined with that scent was another. Softer, floral, feminine. Revi's hackles raised, and he dropped from his perch and loped to the front gate. They weren't near yet, just a teasing aroma on the air.

The aroma of prey, one corner of his mind whispered—the bestial, carnal corner that was always too present these days. Good for hunting. Easy to bring down, to rip his fangs into. He growled and tore his mind away from that line of thought.

He might be trapped in beast form, but he couldn't give in to that side of him. He was beast enough without adding the slaughter of innocents to his sins.

He was still grappling with the desire to *hunt* when the temptation itself arrived at his gate. He sheltered in the shadow of a looming tree, its boughs drooping despite the recent rains, as he studied the small group.

The first thing he saw was *her*. She wore a long-sleeved dress—wool, by the scent of it—that hugged her every curve and was made to protect from the harshest of winters. It was exactly the sort of thing that would have suited his Court, though the Elyri of the Winter Court reveled in the cold.

Sweat dripped down her cheek near her hairline. A cloak to match her dress lay across her saddle and knees. Her cheeks were flushed red from the heat, but her hair shone like spun gold, pushed over one shoulder to keep it off her neck. Her eyes glimmered a deep green, the same shade as winter evergreens that always looked brighter for the snow around it. He would never have mistaken her for an Elyri, not with her curves and round ears, but still she was stunning. More stunning than he had ever thought a human could be.

As an afterthought to her, the leader who'd stolen Revi's frostrose sat atop his own horse, tension making him stiff. Revi could see the resemblance between the two. She had his nose, shared his eyes. He'd brought his own daughter, then.

They stood at the gate for a moment before the man dismounted and approached, walking forward and shaking the obsidian bars with one vigorous shove.

"Beast!" he called. "Prince!" Revi didn't imagine the way the man's lip curled up at the word. "We have come as per our bargain."

Revi prowled forth from the shadows of the tree. The instant the young woman laid eyes on him—a feline as tall as her waist—her beautiful golden skin blanched. Good. At least she wasn't a fool. She knew a predator when she saw one.

He moved closer, and though her lip quivered for just a breath, she mastered herself and clenched her jaw, tilting it up and staring at him with a serene expression. Not quite defiance, but there was steel there. He couldn't help but admire that.

She slid from her horse and stopped before the gate. Her father shifted, partially blocking Revi's view of the woman as if that could stop Revi from taking her.

"I have adhered to my end of the bargain, Winter Prince," the man said, his voice deep and scratchy. "I have brought my daughter, Kienna."

"And I will honor mine." Revi shifted his gaze to the woman. This close, he could better discern her scent. Floral, almost like his frostroses, with an edge of spice like pepper, as well as a hint of spring—turned earth and new growth. She smelled delectable. Revi clamped down on his thoughts again. "She may enter," he said flatly, his tail lashing behind him as he turned away from the gate. "You may not. Come back in a year and a day to fetch her."

The father started to protest. "I can't just abandon her at the gate—"

Revi whipped around and growled. "I said *go*."

The man flinched back, and Kienna watched Revi with wide eyes. If Enlo were here, he would be giving Revi a look, quietly mocking and chiding him simultaneously for losing his temper. He huffed, trying to regain a sense of equilibrium. "I will honor my word that she will be safe, but no other humans are welcome in the heart of my realm. Leave now before my patience runs out."

For the first time, Kienna spoke. "It seems it already has." She smiled at her father in what Revi could only describe as a mollifying sort of way. "It's all right, Papa," she murmured. "He won't hurt me, according to the conditions of his own bargain." She cast a glance in Revi's direction, though she didn't quite meet his gaze. "Isn't that right, Winter Prince?"

"As I have already said." He grew weary of placating these human feelings, but he tried to keep his tone even. "You will be safe here so long as you maintain your side of the bargain."

Her mouth creased down into a frown. "And what does that entail?"

"Stay here, at the Winter Court, for a year and a day." His tail flicked. "Don't touch my frostroses." His tail flicked back the other way. "Don't harm any of my people." His tail flicked back. It felt like the slow dripping of his patience as it ran thinner every moment.

She placed a hand on her father's arm. "See? Nothing so terrible."

His expression softened as he looked at his daughter. He turned back to Revi with fierceness burning in his eyes. "Keep your promise. Protect her with your life."

Revi just stared at him. He'd already said he would. The man was lucky Revi wasn't taking insult to the man doubting his word. *Again.*

Kienna tugged on her father's arm, pulling him away from the gate. Revi edged away as they embraced and murmured to each other. He could hear them, but he had no interest in human sentiment. It was bad enough he'd have to endure her for a year to appease Enlo while he continued to look for his own way to break the curse—even if she was beautiful and had a steely determination.

After several minutes, Kienna turned back to the gate. Her green eyes shone with unshed tears, but she looked at Revi with a steadiness he envied.

"I'm ready."

"*Okryno*," Revi murmured. The gate swung open on silent hinges.

He moved to the side as she stepped forward, a saddlebag in her arms. As soon as she was clear of the gate, he spoke the closing word. It swung shut behind her. The crashing sound made her jump, and she looked back at it with wide eyes. Her hands tightened on her bag. She stared at her father, who gripped the gate with white knuckles, before she turned and started with hesitant steps toward Revi.

He turned toward the castle. He had no desire to walk at her pace. He'd find her new maid and send her for the human.

To his surprise, she caught up to him after a moment and matched his pace. His head reached a little higher than her waist; she was not a slight human, but she looked like she'd still break if he so much as batted at her.

They'd reached the front stairs leading to the doors when she cleared her throat. "I brought the rose with me."

He ignored the instinctive anger at the idea of a human possessing his rose. "Keep it until our bargain is complete."

She was silent only another two breaths. "Is there anything else I should know living here? Any other conditions to the bargain? Or... not formal parts of the bargain, but rather, anything that would make this stay easier on everyone?"

Revi missed a step. He had expected her to put on a brave face in front of her father. He had also thought that once she was alone with him, she would want nothing more than to retreat to her own space. Not to look at him. Not to speak to him. Certainly not to ask questions on how best to collaborate for the duration of her stay. Her bravery ran deeper than he'd expected.

Enlo's needling voice came to the back of his mind.

"It would be in good form if we—" He hated how uncertain his voice sounded. The rest of the words came out in a growl. "If we dined together every night. And spent time together during the days occasionally."

"Every..." She trailed off. "All right," she said, not quite grimacing but doing an admirable job hiding her fear, though she couldn't hide it from her scent, and it set him on edge. "Anything else?"

His nostrils flared. She smelled so good even with that spring-like hint to her scent—his thoughts cut off as recognition poured into him. He snarled and prowled toward her. Alarm flashed across her face, and she stumbled back several steps.

"Where is it?" he snarled. "Where's your elven magic?"

Her eyes widened. "My—"

"You have something made by elves. It reeks of their magic. Drop it on the floor."

Wordlessly, she reached into her skirts and withdrew a smooth blue stone. Revi studied it. He hadn't seen a stone like that in a *very* long time.

"*Razkrys.*"

Magic flared through the stone, revealing its workings to him. Something related to communication, probably over great distances. He huffed out the stink of elven magic, like a breath of spring growth and rich earth, from his nose.

"You may not keep that while you stay."

27

"It was a gift," she said, her voice soft, almost timid.

"Nevertheless," he growled. "Leave it there on the floor. Someone will come collect it." He turned away and started walking again.

She only hesitated briefly before she followed him. The scent of the elven magic receded. Good. She hadn't tried to pick it up again.

"You smell magic?" she asked after a moment, her voice wavering but lanced with curiosity.

"I can smell a great many things."

When they reached the door to the castle, it swung open. Her steps faltered behind him.

"Is there anything else I need to know?"

He didn't answer.

Beyond the door, a young Elyri woman waited. She was lithe and small, a full head shorter than Kienna. At the arrival of her prince and the human, she dropped into a deep bow. He didn't know her name, he realized. He should have asked Enlo for it.

"This is your maid. If you need anything, she'll help you."

The Elyri woman straightened and then bowed again.

Kienna gave her a small smile. "I'm Kienna."

The woman blinked and cast a glance at Revi. "My... my prince... I don't speak this language."

He frowned. Of course she didn't. She was not one of the nobles gifted with language as a child or an ambassador to other Courts, but she would need to be able to communicate with Kienna. Silently, he approached the young woman and pressed his nose to her hand.

"*Zenovor.*" The magic left him in a sudden whoosh, the feeling akin to being kicked in the chest. He dug his claws into the marble floor to steady himself, but still his legs swayed beneath him.

Kienna took a half step forward. "Are you all right?" she asked, her voice almost concerned.

The Elyri woman's eyes widened as she realized what he had done. "I will bear your gift with honor, my prince," she murmured, bowing deeply.

Revi lashed his tail, ill at ease with her gratitude. "Just take care of the woman. She's your charge. Help her with whatever she needs."

"Yes, my prince." The woman turned to Kienna and switched to Kasmian Common like she'd been born speaking it. "Welcome to the Winter Court, my lady."

Kienna's eyebrow tilted up, and she grinned. "You do speak Common. I was worried for a moment."

The woman stole a glance at Revi but said nothing.

"My name is Kienna. What's yours?"

"Zoya," the maid said, barely hesitating at Kienna's bold, thoughtless question; humans didn't know how personal it was to ask an Elyri for their name. "Come, my lady. I'll show you to your quarters."

Kienna nodded but she cast another glance at Revi. "Is there anything else I should know while I stay here, Winter Prince?"

Irritation flared under Revi's skin. "Yes." The word came out as a guttural growl. "Don't ask any more questions. And don't call me Winter Prince."

Kienna's brow shot up, and Zoya's eyes widened.

"What would you rather I call you?" Kienna asked.

Revi didn't know the answer to that. He only knew that every time she called him Winter Prince, it grated under his skin. It felt like a mockery. It was the Winter Court only in name—there was no winter left in his home.

"Nothing. Call me nothing."

"That's ridiculous," Kienna snapped, losing her composure for the first time. "You can't expect me to call you nothing."

"Then pick something else," he growled. "Just do not call me that."

"Well, why don't I call you Beast, then?"

"Perfect. It's fitting." With the irritation of her under his skin and the tantalizing smell of her in his nostrils urging him to act on his predatorial hunting instincts, he felt like little more than a beast. He moved away, leaving the human with her maid.

"I'll see you at dinner, Beast," she called after him, something like a taunt edging her voice.

CHAPTER 5
REVI

R evi retreated to the library after leaving Kienna with her maid. The door was ajar, as most doors in the castle were. Revi could open them, but it was easier not to have to try to deal with the latch.

But *this* open door gave him pause. There was a sense of anticipation to it. It was too inviting. He sniffed the air wafting from the room. A hint of frost and evergreen.

Of course. He sighed and pushed past the door.

Enlo straightened in his seat where he waited on the sofa as soon as Revi entered. "Well? Has she come?"

Revi padded into the room and settled on the rug next to the fireplace. The cold, empty fireplace. They hadn't had to light a fire for anything besides cooking since the curse had begun. His chest tightened with pain at the thought.

"She came. She's with Zoya. I sent her father away already."

Enlo leaned back on the sofa, a look of supreme satisfaction on his face. After a moment, it turned into a sly grin. "Is she beautiful?"

It rankled Revi to admit to Enlo how attractive he found Kienna, so he gave an awkward shrug with one shoulder and looked into the empty fireplace.

Enlo chuckled. "I'll take that as a yes. Oh, this will be such fun. I can't wait to get acquainted with her."

Something in Enlo's tone made Revi's fur stand on end. He cast a slitted glance Enlo's way. "She's not a toy."

Enlo shifted. "I know that. I know her importance. Don't think I will do anything to get in the way of that, cousin."

Revi forced himself to calm. Of course Enlo knew that. He was the one who had pushed Revi into this. And yet he lounged there, carefree and as charming as ever. Something small and tight twisted in Revi's chest. Even if he wanted her to, he didn't think it was possible for a human to fall in love with a creature like him... But Enlo? He was lithe, handsome, an impeccable specimen of an Elyri man. Before the curse, he and Revi could have passed for twins, except for Revi's broader build and longer hair. And, of course, Enlo's infinitely superior personality. Enlo could easily destroy any small chance there was of Kienna falling in love with Revi. Why would a beautiful woman pick a beast when she could have Enlo?

Revi looked away from his cousin. "I know," he conceded. He hesitated and shifted, kneading his paws into the carpet. "That's why I must ask you to stay clear of her."

Enlo laughed. The sound quieted slowly as he realized Revi's seriousness. He was silent so long that Revi stole a glance at him.

He was studying Revi, expression shrewd. Of course he knew exactly what Revi was thinking, but he had the grace not to voice it.

"Very well."

Revi braced himself. "That also means not joining us for dinner."

At that Enlo bristled. He opened his mouth and then snapped it shut with a click of his teeth. This time the smile he gave looked a little bit more like a baring of fangs. "What's missing a few dinners. For a *year*. I'll just eat in the kitchen with the staff."

Revi sank his claws deeper into the carpet, but before he could say anything else, Enlo stood. "It's a wise suggestion, cousin. Of course I'll honor it. I, Enloras, will not seek out the human." The words threaded with the magic that always accompanied a promise made with a name.

Any animosity that Revi had almost certainly imagined vanished as Enlo gave Revi another sly grin. "I'm glad to see you're taking this so seriously. I look forward to hearing all about how the wooing goes."

Revi swallowed a growl. He had no illusions about how any *wooing* would go. He'd rather have to fight a hundred *zruyeds*.

CHAPTER 6
REVI

Kienna was already waiting when Revi reached the dining room that evening. He could smell her from the hallway. Her spicy floral notes—and her fear. It raked against his beast instincts.

Might as well get it over with. Revi stalked into the room. Kienna sat near the end of the table where dishes of food had already been laid out. It wasn't a full feast by Elyri standards—the dwindling food stores wouldn't allow that, but there was more than usual. It seemed the chef wanted to impress the human.

Zoya hovered near the wall behind her.

"You may leave," Revi snapped in their tongue, and Zoya dropped to a quick bow and hurried from the room. Kienna watched her go with wide eyes. He could hear her swallow as she switched her gaze to him, then her sharp intake of breath. He prowled the length of the room, catching his reflection in the dark windows that spanned one wall. A giant silver-white wolf stared back, his eyes—not those of the canine, but of an Elyri or human—glowing a silvery, icy blue.

He jerked his head away from the reflection and looked back at Kienna. Zoya had taken mercy on her and dressed her in a light dress with short bell sleeves. She was just as gorgeous in the summer dress as she had been in her winter one, and she still smelled of that delicious floral, spicy scent without the tang of elven magic on the tail end of it.

Revi hopped onto the sofa that was pushed up to the head of the table in lieu of the normal chair. Monstrously large beasts did not fit well in normal chairs.

"You were a frostcat," Kienna said faintly. He didn't miss the way her pulse throbbed in her neck in time with the pulses of fear in her scent. "And now you're..."

"Not?" he supplied when it seemed like she wouldn't be finishing that sentence.

"Do you have a... human form? Or the fae equivalent? Like Zoya?"

He wrestled with the sharp ache her question produced. Until the curse was broken, the answer to that was a harsh negative. Before the curse, he'd been as much of a man as Enlo, but he'd frequently shifted into animal forms when they suited his purposes; it was another layer of insult to the Summer Queen's curse that she'd trapped him in the forms he'd once chosen for himself. The truth of it mocked him; it felt too humiliating to admit to a human.

"Is your room to your taste?" The cordial question was awkward on his lips, awkward in the air since it was a blatant disregard of her own questions. It had been so long since he had had to make small talk. It had been so long since he'd had anyone but Enlo or the small staff who stayed at the castle to talk to. People visited on matters of business—those reporting to him on the state of the Court and their efforts to stave off the curse's impending doom—but those didn't require pleasantries, and they never stayed long. Revi sent them away—away from him and the curse that clung to him. Here, at his castle—or anywhere else he stayed for longer than a few days—the Winter Court was afflicted the worst by the deep throes of summer.

It was paltry, but it was one way he could protect them, and protecting his people was his primary concern. It was what he'd been doing in fighting the *zruyeds* since they'd first appeared years before, and he wouldn't stop now just because his foe was a curse he couldn't fight with blade or claw. He would protect his people to his dying breath.

Kienna nodded, frowning slightly at his avoidance, but she didn't push the previous topic. "It's... it's beautiful." A smile brightened her features as she continued, "And Zoya is truly lovely. Thank you for assigning her to me."

He hummed, and it came out as a soft rumble. Kienna flinched, which only made him want to growl further. This wasn't one of his people, familiar with his ways. Or at least better at hiding their discomfort.

"Shall we?" He cast a pointed glance at the covered dishes.

"Oh, of course." Kienna rose from her seat to reach across the table to lift the covers protecting the food. Her plate was filled to the brim. Revi pushed back the worry twisting through him. So much food—probably more than she would even eat. A small bowl of creamy soup off to one side smelled of potato, and on the plate itself a little bit of everything was mounded. The staff clearly weren't sure what to feed the human, on top of wanting to impress her. The thought almost made Revi chuckle. The scents wafting off it curled into his nose. They'd made it bland, at least, as per Revi's orders—he remembered the stories of the humans who stayed in Elyri Courts solely because after eating the best food the Elyri had to offer, their own human foods were little better than dirt to them. If Kienna chose to stay, it needed to be because of her feelings for him, not for the food.

In front of Revi, of course, was a large plate of meat chopped in large chunks. His portion, at least, had stayed the same. Good. He didn't need them straining the larders more than they already were for Kienna. It had, unfortunately, been seared on the edges and sides so it didn't just look like it had been pulled from the butcher's block. Revi preferred it raw, but he had accepted a long time ago that his chef thought it was undignified for his prince to eat like a beast in front of other people. Which meant Revi's meat was far more cooked than he liked to eat it these days.

He braced himself for it. The kitchen was only doing what they thought would help ingratiate him to the woman. They wanted the curse over as much as Enlo. He would eat it, somehow, and he would look forward to going hunting soon for fresh meat.

As if stirred by the thought, the quiet predator in his mind pointed out he had fresh meat right beside him, but he shoved it away and bit into the seared steak before him. Hesitantly following suit, Kienna picked up a spoon and dipped it into her soup. They ate in silence, Revi uncomfortably aware of the human.

He tried to be delicate as he forced down the cooked meat, but all that served to do was make him look clumsy as he dropped several pieces back onto the plate and one even onto the floor. A growl erupted from him at that.

Kienna watched him wrestle with his food. She bent over and stabbed the piece on the floor with her fork and offered it back to him. He only stared at it and then at her, and she rested it on his plate instead.

"You don't yet seem used to eating as an animal," she said. "How long have you been like this?"

He cast a sharp look at her. "Been like what?"

37

"A... a beast." At his flat look, she huffed and rolled her eyes. "It's painfully obvious there's something wrong here. You can't expect me not to notice it. You only take the forms of animals, and perhaps that's perfectly normal for fae, but I'm fairly certain that the Winter Court being in the midst of a droughty summer is *definitely* unusual."

Revi held back the snarl that wanted to rip from him. He had no intention of telling her the curse, but he had neglected to consider whether anyone else would have the same sense.

"Did Zoya tell you something she ought not?" The words came out more growling than he intended.

Kienna's eyebrows puckered together. "No. She was very friendly, but if I tried to ask her anything about it, she shut up like a pinecone."

Revi leaned back. At least there was that small grace. He would have to speak to Zoya to ensure she continued to keep her silence.

"What is wrong with your Court?" Kienna pressed. "Is that why I'm here? Something to do with it?"

He snapped up another piece of meat in front of him, not caring any longer if it disturbed her. "This falls under the purview of questions, little human," he finally said.

She stabbed at the leafy greens on her plate with too much force, clinking the plate beneath. "Then I suppose asking why the castle is empty would as well," she said, her voice tense. "Why you have no family or court in your Winter Court." She stopped and drew in a deep breath as if trying to calm herself. When she looked at him again, there was understanding in her eyes, but that only made Revi's hackles raise. "If only you would tell me, I'd be willing to help. Secrets serve no one but themselves. If you would just—"

He snarled, and she cut off, flinching away.

"Your human mind is ill prepared to understand all I have endured. All I've had to do. All those I have hurt."

She flinched again at his guttural tone.

He rose and stepped down from the seat, stalking behind her chair and pushing his muzzle closer to her side. He could hear her rapid pulse, smell her rising fear. It made the predator in him hungry, especially after that paltry attempt at nourishment.

"Telling you won't fix anything," he continued, his voice a deep growl. "There's—" His voice choked off, his Elyri magic not allowing him to finish the lie. Instead of trying to come up with a truth that would keep her from questioning him further, he turned and stalked from the room.

CHAPTER 7
ENLO

E nlo ripped himself from his magic, coming to in his bed and sitting up with a jerk. He didn't have as much magic as Revi, but he'd long since perfected the Winter Elyri skill of soulwalking—sending his spirit beyond his body to spy and learn things he would never know otherwise. It was invaluable in the politics of court, but he hadn't needed it recently—not before Kienna's arrival. The temptation to lurk and watch the first dinner between Revi and the human had been too much for him. And now that he had...

Fury was lightning in his veins. How could Revi have been so stupid? Enlo had hoped that the reticence he'd sensed in his cousin when he and Revi had discussed breaking the curse via Kienna's affections had been his imagination. Or, if not that, then at least that Revi wouldn't let his reservations hinder him when it came to actually wooing the human.

Enlo had clearly hoped in vain.

If Revi was ever going to sway the human's heart, snarling at her and scaring her away from helping was not the path forward. Enlo curled his fingers into a fist, his slightly pointed, clawed nails digging into his palm. If Revi was left to his own devices, they would all die before the curse was broken.

If only Enlo could take Revi's place. Before the curse, he had never wanted for female companionship. Women loved his easy smile and charismatic nature. If it were left to him, he would have already had the human blushing.

What if... what if it *were* up to him? The idea unfurled in his mind slowly, a banner of impossibility and hope. He was not the Winter Prince. He was not the ruler of their Court. But he *was* from the royal family. Maybe, just maybe, that would be enough to satisfy the curse... And if he could break the curse, he would. In a heartbeat. Revi was like his brother, but Revi was too coiled up in his own pride, his own bitterness, to do what needed to be done.

Revi would kill them all.

The thought left an acrid tinge at the back of his throat, but he brushed it away. Revi was suited to war; Enlo was suited to the people, especially to women. It was just their natures. It wasn't disloyal of him to acknowledge Revi's weakness. He only wanted to help their Court. For Revi. For their people. For him. He was so *tired* of this awful slow dying of the life he'd known.

Still, he would say nothing to his cousin, not until he had researched and studied the curse further to ensure it was a real possibility. There was no need to give false hope. He closed his eyes and pictured the human: her golden hair, the way that summery lilac dress had hugged her curves. She lacked the elegant pointed ears of the Elyri, the sharp glint of cunning in her eyes, the angular jaw and cheekbones, but she was beautiful in her own way. Soft curves, sweetness like a ripe piece of fruit. There was an innocence to her.

Yes. Enlo's mouth curved into a slow smile. He was confident that he could steal the girl's heart.

CHAPTER 8
REVI

"**A**nd the caves?"

Revi's steward, a diminutive Elyri man with glittering grey eyes and dark hair the exact shade of green as a fir's needles, scratched the side of his nose. "No new reports, Your Highness. Our men are still scouting them to ensure their safety."

Revi huffed. He resisted the urge to rub his muzzle against his paw; just because he looked like a wolf didn't mean he needed to act like one before his steward. "Very well. You may go. Take the Spring Court's trade proposal to Enlo; he'll write up a response to them." Something far more civil than Revi could manage, given that the new trade proposal not only rejected their request for more food imports but also said the Spring King intended to cut back their shipments—*and* raise the taxes.

If they didn't desperately need the food, Revi would have shredded the whole thing. It was insulting.

Restless and frustrated after such a fruitless morning, Revi abandoned the library. He needed some quiet, some time to gather his patience about him before he dealt with anything else for his Court today. A visit to his frostroses would help.

He stepped out of a side door into the sun, which glared down across the gardens. A few wispy clouds drifted through the sky, the only remnants of the rainstorm that had visited the night before.

Revi lifted his nose to the air and inhaled. A familiar scent came to him on the breeze, and he growled. What was the woman doing out here? Did she think to take another rose like her father had? He hadn't seen much of her in the past week aside from dinners—which were rather quiet affairs, overall. They stayed on polite conversation topics, with Kienna occasionally asking him what the Elyri words for things were. But during the days, he only caught glimpses of her, often with Zoya.

He followed the scent, his suspicion growing as the trail led him closer to his personal garden. He'd let her keep that one rose as a sign of the bargain struck, but if she dared take another of his roses...

He stopped in his tracks when she came into sight around a bend in the path.

Kienna knelt a short distance away by one of the flower beds, pouring a pitcher of water on a wilting flower bush. Her dress trailed in the dust around her, not that she seemed to notice.

She clutched the pitcher in her hands, a drop of water rolling down its side. The ground around the bush before her looked wet.

He stared, unsure what to do with the sight of her.

After a moment, she rose to her feet and stepped back onto the path. A frown marred her face as she contemplated the bush. When she turned back to the castle, she started at the sight of Revi; pink flooded her cheeks. "Were you watching me?"

He moved forward, tilting his head toward the bush. "We have gardeners to do that."

Her fingers tightened on the pitcher, and her gaze flicked to the bush. "I just thought... they're probably very busy with the entire grounds. And perhaps wouldn't mind a little help." Her brow furrowed as she studied the plant. "I don't understand why the plants struggle here. It rained last night—stormed, even. I heard it pounding against my window." She looked back at him, her eyes searching his. "Why does your Court look like it's in the middle of a drought?"

He shifted, kneading his claws into the ground as he grappled for an answer. He didn't know what to do with this strange woman who seemed to care so much. Yes, she was living here for a year, but this was not her Court. She didn't know that its future rested on her.

She continued, unaware of the direction of his thoughts, "When my father came home with that rose, I expected this place to be vibrant. Instead, it's..." She waved a hand out toward the struggling flora.

"Why do you care?" He prowled forward a step as the questions burned out of him. "What is it to you the state my Court is in? Shouldn't you be pleased that your captor is in such dire straits?"

"No." She shook her head, her hands twisting around the pitcher's handle. "Why would I be? I wouldn't wish this plight on anyone. Even if I don't entirely know what the plight is."

The fervency in her tone was startling. How could she care so much for a place she'd only been for a week?

Her gaze trailed back to the browning bush, and her next words were soft. Perhaps not meant for his ears, but of course he heard them anyway. "Is there nothing in your Court still thriving?"

He frowned, taken aback by the sudden desire to comfort her, to prove all was not entirely lost yet. He could—he *would*—still fix this somehow. Protect his people. He'd even do it without her help. He didn't need her. Even if he did find her far more intriguing—even... alluring, with her strange propensity to care despite having no reason to—than he'd ever expected to find a human.

"Follow me." He stalked past her, his shoulder brushing her hip. The back of her hand grazed against his side as she fell in beside him, her slippers scuffing softly over the dirt. He was intensely aware of her touch on his fur. She didn't remove her hand, didn't shift away from him.

They walked in silence for a few moments before Revi cleared his throat, the noise more of a growl than any sound a person would make. At *that,* she flinched.

He pretended he hadn't noticed. "Did you enjoy gardening before? In your homeland."

She recovered quickly. "Occasionally. It wasn't my favorite pastime, but I would do it with my mother." She glanced sideways at him. "I'd ask if you do, but I can't really imagine it."

His chest prickled. "Why? Because I'm a beast? I can dig plenty well." He gouged his claws into the earth for emphasis.

She tensed beside him, and a thread of annoyance bled into her voice. "No. I was going to say because you're a prince. As you pointed out yourself, you have people to tend the grounds for you."

"...Oh." He started walking again.

"You know, it doesn't really matter what you look like." Her voice was timid, and her fear contradicted her, but as he gave her another sideways glance, she warmed to her topic. Even the fear bled away from her scent as she continued, "Just because you look like a wolf"—she gestured to him—"or a giant cat doesn't mean you aren't simply a normal person too. You don't have to act like you're as beastly as you look."

He studied her for a moment, utterly bemused by her words. It was impossible that she believed that. "I'm exactly as beastly as I look, Lady Kienna. You would be wise not to forget it."

"Are you?" The question was quiet. He pretended not to hear it.

"Where are you taking me, anyway?" she asked after a short pause, raising her voice to a normal volume.

He side-eyed her. "You're terrible at keeping to the no questions rule."

Her eyes widened, and then she huffed, a smile tugging at one corner of her mouth. "You started asking questions first. Perhaps you're a bad example."

He blinked. Was she... teasing him? He shook his head and pushed away the confusion of feelings the idea raised in him. "Regardless, here we are."

They turned the last corner in the path, coming around the towering bushes that guarded this side of his garden from view of the castle.

She gasped at the sight before them. She took a few faltering steps forward, her hand raised toward the frostroses, before she froze and shot a glance at Revi.

"I'm sorry," she said. "I know you don't like..."

He pushed down on the possessive feeling rising up in him and shrugged one shoulder. He had brought her here. It made no sense to threaten her off them now.

"Just don't pick any," he said in a low growl.

She nodded her head. "They're even more beautiful in their natural environment."

Revi gave another low growl of agreement.

The bush towered over Kienna's head, blooms bursting from every side of it. In the sea of failing life around them, this was the one explosion of vitality. She slowly circled it, brushing her fingers across every petal they passed.

He felt oddly pleased at her wonder, her delight, as she admired the frostroses from every angle. It was like seeing them anew himself. Perhaps it was just her running her fingers across the petals; he could almost imagine he felt a phantom touch along his shoulders. Maybe he did. These were tied to him, after all. He shivered. It was far too easy for his mind to take the idea of her fingers and expand on it, on how soft her touch would be against his skin.

If he had regular skin. The thought soured it, and he shook the idea away.

When Kienna returned to his side of the bush, her brow was creased in another frown. "These are beautiful. But... how can they thrive when the rest of your Court is dying?"

Revi shifted. "These will always survive while I'm alive. They're a manifestation of my magic. In a way, they're an extension of me, and I of them. My magic flows from it, and into it, keeping it strong."

Her eyes widened, and her hand froze on a rose. She looked back and forth between him and the bush. Her hand drew back slowly. "Do all fae have a special rosebush?"

"No." He padded closer and nudged a flower with his nose. The leaves nearby tickled his whiskers. "Only Elyri from the royal family—those directly in line for the throne—have their magic manifest in a physical form. And it's not always roses. My father has a pine, my mother moss."

Kienna looked around, as if she expected to see those nearby.

"They're closer to the front of the castle. But they don't stand out as much as the frostroses." His hide prickled at the painful reminder. "Come. I have duties to attend to."

She nodded, grazing her fingers across a large rose one last time before they started back toward the castle.

"Thank you," she said after a few minutes, "for showing me these. Perhaps if they can survive this strange drought thanks to you, the rest of your Court will too."

His steps faltered as he looked up at her. She gave him a small smile, a dimple forming on one cheek, before hurrying ahead.

He watched her go, his thoughts tilting in her wake. She was just a human.

And yet he found himself encouraged by her words. By her belief in him, however superficial. He didn't need her to fix his curse—but he wanted to get to know her better, to understand how she could give her belief and kindness so freely.

Yet she still flinched when he growled. Wisps of fear still swirled with her scent when she was reminded of his beastliness. And he couldn't blame her. Who wouldn't flinch? Who would want to converse with an animal? Bitterness welled in him.

If he wanted to get to know her, he'd have to do so beyond his cursed forms. And there was only one way to do that.

CHAPTER 9
REVI

As soon as Revi fell asleep, he reached for his magic. Dreamwalking was not a skill unique to him, but only the strongest Winter Elyri could harness their magic in such a way. Enlo had often bemoaned how difficult he found it to connect to others while they slept, much less walk through their dreams. If he were better at it, he would use it to spy on people and learn their secrets, as he did with his soulwalking. Revi had no patience for such machinations.

But when the Summer Queen had cursed him, she had cursed his body only, not his mind. Which meant that if he wanted to get closer to Kienna, to get to know her without her fear of his beastly nature creating a wall between them, dreamwalking was the only way he could do so. It wasn't easy—it pulled at his magic and left him fatigued, but it felt necessary.

He took a moment to orient himself to the body he naturally wore in this dream world—his true form, that of an Elyri man. He could take whatever form he wanted in dreams, but this was the only place—the only time—he could be himself. So he left his appearance alone, doing nothing to his long silver hair and blue eyes. He looked just like Enlo, except for the hair and a broader build, thanks to Revi's years of training and fighting. Enlo had chosen to spend his years training his mind and charms far more than his warrior skills.

Enlo and Revi perfectly balanced each other, Enlo used to say. He rooted out the enemies within the Court while Revi conquered the ones beyond.

At least until Revi's own pride had brought the Summer Queen's wrath upon them. Revi couldn't conquer his curse with claw or blade.

He pushed away the familiar anger and focused on the dream world around him. Everything was swathed in darkness, the minds of those nearby scattered about like stars. He walked amongst them, focusing briefly on each one he passed, searching for the familiar notes of Kienna. Her scent, her voice, anything. The minds of people didn't always manifest in the same way in this dream world; when he focused on a star, he might hear their whispers, or he might feel a sensation against his fingertips. It varied from person to person, and it could even vary from night to night. If he found Kienna's dreams by her scent tonight, he might find it by her laugh tomorrow.

Finally, he drew close to a star, and the sensations of a soft touch and a flicker like sunlight on golden hair pulled him forward. He touched the star, and a world burst into being around him.

Kienna's dream was a cozy cottage, with cob walls and a thatched roof. It was nestled amidst trees in a forest not unlike the Winter Court's conifers. The heat of the curse pressed down here, too. Its presence loomed too much to even be escaped in dreams.

Revi crossed the tiny clearing just in front of the cottage's door. There was a window with shutters to the left of the door and a window in the wooden door itself, this one with a curtain that fluttered in a faint breeze. Even with his regular sense of hearing—still better than that of a human's—Revi could hear Kienna moving about within, her footsteps barely audible on the packed dirt floor. A soft clatter followed—porcelain against wood, probably.

He raised his hand and knocked. The sounds stopped.

And then she moved, and the curtain brushed to the side, and he was staring into her green eyes, confusion tilting her brows slightly.

They stared at each other for a long moment. Revi shifted. The primary rule of dreamwalking was that one couldn't truly enter a dream without permission. He was here, yes, but unless she invited him in, he would never gain entrance to her inner sanctuary—the cottage itself. And if she asked him to leave, he would be forced from the dream entirely.

He pitched his voice low and soft. "Won't you let me in?"

"I..." Her throat bobbed, her gaze flicking over his face and back to his eyes as some internal debate warred within her.

She was going to turn him away. Somehow she knew, even when he looked like a prince instead of the beast he was—she knew his true nature.

Kienna shook her head, and the creak of the doorknob came. She pulled open the door and stepped aside for Revi to enter. He did so quickly, relief washing over him. He swept past her and took one of the two chairs at the table. Two teacups already waited on the table, as if she'd been expecting him.

The door clicked shut, and Kienna moved past him, rubbing her forehead as she leaned over the fire where the tea kettle was just beginning to whistle an inviting tune.

She grabbed it off the fire, freezing only after she was halfway to the table. Her eyes widened and took in that she had no rag to protect her from its metal handle.

"It won't hurt you," Revi said. "This is your dream. You're safe from most things here."

Her gaze jerked up to him.

"Truly." He offered a small smile he hoped was reassuring. He didn't have much practice smiling these days. Not that he'd had much before the curse, either.

She stood frozen a moment longer, still grappling with the wholly unnatural concept of feeling no pain, before she swallowed again and shifted back into motion, pouring steaming water into the teacups.

Revi watched her closely. Despite the heat here, she wore a dress of wool—finely made, but still simple, and human in design. It suited her; perhaps she was simply more comfortable in the style than she was in the Elyri-made dresses he had provided for her.

She set a teacup in front of him and took the seat across from him, drawing the other teacup closer to herself. His finger brushed the handle of the cup, but he did not drink. He only continued to watch her.

"What brings you to my cottage?" She traced a finger along the rim of her cup and studied him as openly as he studied her, taking in his hair, his eyes, his princely Elyri tunic and trousers, the fine silver circlet on his brow. She seemed impressed by what she saw—so much so that he almost regretted coming. Had he truly thought letting her get to know him in a dream would help anything? At best, he'd get her to fall in love with him here, as the curse wanted, but then she'd just be horrified when she learned the truth of his identity—that the prince before her was just a facade for the beast she knew in the waking world. It would do nothing to break the curse.

Nothing but her choosing to see him as more than a beast—despite that being exactly what he was—would.

"You mustn't trust your eyes," he said abruptly, his frustration snapping out. The sharpness of his tone made her draw back a little.

"Why not?"

"You must not trust your eyes," he repeated, "for they are easily deceived."

She tucked her hair behind her ear and shifted in her seat. Curiosity swirled around her, and it was almost alluring, given its total absence of fear. It had been so long since anyone besides Enlo had looked at him without at least a trace of fear. "If you could only tell me why, sir, this conversation would be much more productive."

Instead of answering, he took a deep swallow of tea. It should have scalded his throat, but he ignored the nudging in his mind of the idea, and it quickly faded away.

"What's your name?" she asked.

His gaze shot up to hers; then he grimaced and looked away, making some of his hair fall over his shoulder. She wasn't asking for his true name. She just wanted something to call him, as she had before when she had first arrived in the Winter Court. She just didn't know what an intimate question she asked.

Either way, he found he didn't want to give her a name that could be tied to him in the waking world, not even his shortened name—and he couldn't give her a false name.

"Do you like your new home?" he asked instead.

She smiled. "Of course I do. Everything is so… fine." She trailed off as she looked around her warm, cozy cottage—rustic and pleasant, but by no means fine. She shook her head. "I'm sorry. What was the question?"

Revi sighed. Clearly the confusion of the dream state was still pressing on her mind. "Do you like your new home in the waking world?"

At those words, her eyes cleared, as he'd expected they would. Once one realized they were in a dream, it became far easier to navigate it.

"Oh. Oh. It's very beautiful," she said. "I've never seen anything quite like it. Are you from the waking world? Do you live in the castle too?"

He grimaced but nodded.

She rested her chin on the heel of her hand. "Do you have a bargain with the beast, too?"

He flinched and stood, setting his teacup down hard enough to slosh a little tea over the side. He'd reached his limit for this charade of pretending he wasn't exactly what he was: the beast in question. But perhaps he could nudge her to at least consider staying on the right course in the waking world. "Keep your bargain. Spend time with the beast, and perhaps you can free us from our cruel misery."

Her brow furrowed. "Of course I will. I've already agreed to it."

"Then perhaps all hope is not lost," he muttered.

"Do you know why he wants me to stay for a year?" Her eyes pinned to him, bright and hopeful.

"I think it's time for you to wake up now." He locked gazes with her and reached out, running his fingers down her cheek and pushing her from the dream.

Of course, doing so threw him out of the space as well, and he jerked upright in his own bed, back in his quarters in the castle. He groaned, the sound coming out as more of a growl—because here he was not himself; he was a monstrously large frostcat. He huffed and dropped back to his belly.

It had felt good to be back in his own form for a little while.

And, he admitted quietly to himself, seeing Kienna smile at him, speaking to him without an edge of fear to every word—that had been a balm on his soul. Even as it frustrated him.

He didn't know yet if he would go back and visit her dreams again in his true form. His original plan of using it to get to know her was a foolish one. To break the curse, she needed to love the beast in the waking world, not the false prince in her dreams.

But he might return. Not to woo her; he didn't want her help breaking the curse anyway. Maybe he would go—just to be greeted warmly. To bask quietly in her kindness.

Perhaps he had left the dream too soon. He settled into the soft bedding, his heart quickening as he recalled the softness of her face under his fingertips.

CHAPTER 10

REVI

He didn't have the magical reserves to return to her dreams again, but Revi found himself seeking Kienna out in the real world in the following days.

No, not seeking her out. He just happened to want to spend time in the library when she was there. Every single afternoon that week.

He had a lot of reading he wanted to do.

Today he sat in wolf form, on his preferred sofa, a book across his large paws. But while his eyes were trained on the page, his ears were attuned to Kienna's every movement.

He hadn't tried to speak to her. She'd tensed that first day when he came in, but he'd given her a brief nod and then—as far as she could tell—ignored her. So she'd ignored him, even if fear still lingered in the air. They'd spent their days like that. Him reading—or pretending to—and taking care of any Court business his steward brought to him. Kienna read or, if Zoya was there, asked her maid questions about Elyri culture and language. She seemed frustrated by their limited collection of books written in Kasmian Common, so she'd set herself the task of learning Elyri instead. Revi briefly considered gifting her the language with his magic, as he had for Zoya, but he quickly discarded the idea. If she didn't end up staying, he had no desire to give her a tactical advantage over his Court by knowing the language as fluently as an Elyri. And if she could read the language, she could read the curse inscribed on the scroll laid out under the window. That wouldn't help anyone.

But... if she cared enough to learn it herself, he wouldn't stop her. Maybe her eagerness was a promising sign.

She asked dozens of questions, and Zoya humored her, though she seemed hesitant to answer Kienna when Revi was present. It was like she was nervous around him.

But when he didn't bite her head off for teaching Kienna how to read the Elyri alphabet from a children's book, she relaxed. And Kienna did too.

The maid was good for something after all.

And slowly, as he showed up every afternoon—along with their dinners every evening—the fear faded into the background until it was so faint it stopped calling to the predator lurking in Revi's mind. The silence became almost companionable. He found himself sitting, eyes closed, just listening to the peace of the library. Being with another person, without any demands on him, without any fear tainting the air—he'd forgotten how restorative that felt.

"Can I ask you something?" Kienna broke the silence for the first time since he'd entered that day.

Revi's gaze flicked to her for half a second before he forced it back to his page, as if he'd been reading. He hadn't, but she didn't need to know that. He relished that she had spoken to him, and he spoke the first thing that came to mind. "You will regardless of how I answer that."

The words came out more abruptly than he'd meant them, sounding more annoyed than teasing. He cringed internally; he could practically feel Enlo glowering at him. Not that his cousin was present, but if he were, he'd be furious at Revi for being rude to the human.

From the corner of his eye, he saw Kienna's mouth twitch. She was probably withholding a frown.

"I've been rereading this story book—"

"Enjoying it that much, are you?" Revi cut in drily.

She shrugged. "You don't have many books written in Kasmian Common, and sometimes my mind needs a rest from deciphering your Elyri runes. Anyway. I've been reading this one, with its stories about Elyri Courts. And this story." She tapped the page.

"'She pressed him for his loyalties, fear crippling her breaking heart
When she asked him who he stood beside—with whom he chose to plot
Jormun's tongue ached to betray the truth, as tongues are wont to do
He wrapped a hand round his throat in a last bid to keep his secrets true.'"

Kienna looked up at Revi. Her eyes were bright, fetching in a way that made Revi want to lean closer to her, to run his hands through her hair. If he had hands, if he weren't a cursed beast.

"This makes it sound like Jormun didn't even have a choice in speaking the truth," she said.

"Where's the question?" Revi asked, finally wrestling his mind off her eyes and hair to focus on her words.

"Can Elyri lie?"

Revi blinked. Clever human. A small rumble rolled from him through the room. "No."

Kienna's eyes narrowed. "How do I know you're not lying about that right now?"

Revi huffed out a laugh. There was nothing he could say that would assure her he wasn't.

"I'll just have to test it." Kienna stood and set her book onto the chair's cushion. Revi leaned away as she approached him, a determined glint to her eye. What was she plotting?

She perched on the end of Revi's sofa, just beyond his book, and peered into Revi's face. This close, he was wholly enveloped by her sweet scent, by how she filled his space with her bright green eyes and mischievous smile.

"What's your name?"

Revi's eyes narrowed. "You call me Beast."

"And yet that's not your name."

"It's a worthy title."

"But it's not your name. Do you not tell me your name because you hate me?"

Revi withheld a grimace. Of course that was the conclusion she'd come to. He was a beast. His every action probably felt threatening.

"I don't hate you," he said stiffly.

Kienna hummed, her eyes twinkling in a charming way. "That sounded like it hurt to say. What *do* you think of me?"

Revi opened his mouth—choked on his words and swallowed. Answering that would only embarrass him. "You're quiet."

"That's a statement of fact, not your opinion."

Revi cast around again. "You... are very attractive." Her eyes widened, and he found himself blurting out the only other thing he could think of to save his pride. To hide his heart behind. "By human standards."

Kienna's lips twitched. "I think that was almost a compliment."

"Are you sufficiently convinced of your theory?" Revi asked gruffly.

Kienna studied him for several moments, making Revi shift. "What's your favorite color?"

Revi blinked. "Why does that matter?"

"Humor me."

"White."

"Favorite food?"

"Meat."

"Do you prefer it raw?"

Revi hesitated.

"You always eat the least-cooked pieces from your plate at dinner." Her tone was level, no hint of the disgust or fear Revi would have expected to accompany such a statement.

"Yes," Revi agreed reluctantly. He could hardly deny it, no matter how he might want to.

She tilted her head. "Why is it cooked at all, then?"

He shifted. "My cook thought it would scare you off if I ate it raw around you."

"You should tell them I don't mind." She gave an encouraging smile at his look of disbelief. "Really. Eat your food how you prefer it. It won't be the strangest thing I've seen here."

It was a tiny thing, but his chest tightened all the same. How could she act so nonchalant about the idea of him taking his meat entirely raw? It was a clear mark of his beastliness.

Kienna, oblivious to his roiling mind, continued her rapid questions. "Favorite time of day?"

He blinked himself out of his thoughts. "Sunset."

"Have you ever met an elf?"

"Not since I was a child."

"Have you ever climbed on the roof of your castle?"

"Of course."

"What's your name?"

"Rev—" He cut off with a growl. He jerked to his feet and jumped from the sofa. "You tricked me."

Kienna tensed, her shoulders coming up around her ears. "On the bright side, if you could lie about your name, I doubt you'd be so angry right now."

The growl that rumbled from him made Kienna flinch, and a faint swirl of fear entered her scent. It stabbed through his frustration, bursting and dispersing it. He didn't want to return to the tension of before, to the way her fear made his beast instincts hungry.

"What's the rest of your name?" she asked, her voice small and nowhere near as confident as it had been a moment before. "Rev-what?"

Revi's hackles were raised. He didn't want to give her his name, either. "It doesn't matter. You'll not call me anything but Beast."

Kienna grimaced and stood. She gave Revi a wide berth as she returned to her chair, closing her book. "As you wish. I think I'll go rest now."

Revi watched her flee and sighed. He might have ruined what peace they'd found, all because he couldn't keep the beast within and out of sight.

CHAPTER 11
ENLO

A s the weeks passed, Enlo never approached Kienna, as promised. That didn't mean he didn't *watch* her, though. She was the first new, interesting thing at the Winter Court since the curse had begun. Revi could hardly expect him not to be curious.

And curious he was. Especially since she took to spending her days in the library, which meant Enlo couldn't spend *his* time in the library. When he wasn't helping run the Court, he kept to his room—physically, at least.

Soulwalking didn't break his promise.

So Enlo saw how Revi lurked in the library with Kienna, though he never used the time to ingratiate himself with her. Enlo saw their quiet days pass, each one wasted. He saw Kienna puzzle out that Elyri couldn't lie—and Revi's infuriating reaction to Kienna almost learning his name. He saw Kienna continue to study the Elyri language with Zoya and reach the point where she could carry a basic conversation.

He watched as she grew more comfortable at the Winter Court. She spent her days either with Zoya or with Revi, in the library or in a parlor, embroidering and sewing. Sometimes she'd visit the gardens, but that always seemed to leave her melancholy.

It grated on Enlo's skin to watch Revi's poor attempts at wooing. Nonexistent would be more accurate. Revi might as well have left her alone for all the good the days together did. Dinners were slightly more talkative, as if both silently agreed that was when they'd make more of an effort to converse, but even that rankled Enlo. Kienna put more effort into their conversations than Revi did. She had accepted her role in the Court for a year, and she was making the best of it. Revi was living life as he had before Kienna's arrival—caring for his people, looking for a way to break the curse.

Ignoring the opportunity right in front of him.

Enlo's resentment toward Revi grew with each day. If *he'd* been in Revi's place, Kienna would already be in love with him.

And of course, Enlo couldn't pursue his studies of what little they knew of their curse while Kienna haunted the library. He was forced to take the one opportunity he had to study when he knew for certain the library would be empty. The dinners may have been short, but it was a guaranteed time when neither Revi nor Kienna would come to the library.

He turned the curse over in his mind, running his fingers over every individual word. *Until the strongest of the weak a lifelong devotion does speak, and restores a Heart of Winter.*

A, not *the*. He tapped the single-lettered word as he weighed it in his thoughts.

An awareness pressed against Enlo, and he snapped the book shut, rising and returning it to the pedestal by the window. The awareness approached, expanded as a whisper of noise sounded from the hallway.

Enlo returned to the sofa, a more innocuous book in hand. He had just opened it when Revi stalked in, as silent as ever. Enlo didn't have to feign his curiosity as he glanced at his cousin. He hadn't been listening in on Revi and Kienna's dinner tonight.

"How was the evening meal?" he asked.

Revi only gave a low noncommittal growl, one that made Enlo want to growl back even though he wasn't an animal like his cousin. Instead, he forced a smile.

"I take it she's practically in love with you." The words grated, but he managed to get them out, for it wasn't a direct lie. Anything could have happened while he'd been preoccupied with his books tonight. He could hold on to the foolish, mad hope that something *had*.

At least until Revi's disbelieving snort filled the air. "No one could ever love me as I am, cousin. I'm a beast."

Enlo tensed, then forced himself to relax. "But what about a charming prince?" he countered.

Revi's growl rippled in the quiet room. "I am not the charming one here. And I have better things to do."

"And I am not the prince," Enlo snapped, frustration boiling over at his cousin's pride.

Revi turned slowly, his piercing blue eyes cutting through Enlo.

Enlo held perfectly still, resisting the urge to run his hands through his hair. If his cousin suspected him for even a moment... Enlo could not allow that. He only wanted what was best for the Court, but would Revi understand that if he could hear Enlo's thoughts?

No. Better to wait a little while longer, until Enlo knew for certain. Enlo forced a lazy smile to his face and threw a hand over the back of the chair.

"You're thinking about this too hard, Revi. You need to stop thinking of yourself as a beast and start thinking instead as a man. A man singularly lucky enough to have the opportunity of a beautiful woman all to himself."

Revi's eyes hardened, and he jerked his gaze away as his tail started lashing.

Enlo wanted to rip at his hair. "You're more than just a beast. You're the prince of our Court, the Heart of Winter." The words burned up his throat as he thought of the curse. *A*, not *the*.

"I may be the Heart of Winter," Revi agreed in a low rumble, "but these forms cannot show the human something that isn't there. To break the curse your way, she will have to love me as a beast." At these words, he scoffed. "Or she will never love me at all. It was a false hope to bring her here."

Enlo's hands clawed into the back of the sofa as his heart cracked in his chest. He had always loved Revi. He had always supported him, stood by him through the tumultuous years since his cousin had taken the throne in his parents' absence. He had protected Revi's back in the war—though he wasn't even half the warrior Revi was. Together, they had driven away their enemies, but now thorns wrapped around Enlo's heart. He had never wished as much as he did in that moment that he was not second to the throne. Second to Revi. Because if that was how Revi saw himself, if that was what he presented to Kienna for her entire stay with them, Enlo's hope of the curse breaking was foolish indeed.

Any trace of doubt in his mind vanished. He could not trust the task of breaking the curse to his cousin. Which meant that Enlo was the Winter Court's only hope.

CHAPTER 12
KIENNA

K ienna woke in her cozy cottage. She stood and looked around at the mismatched furniture, the soft quilt thrown over one chair, the light curtains fluttering from the warm breeze blowing from outside.

She moved to prepare tea. As she did so, she marveled over her familiarity with the space. But of course it was familiar. Her memories whispered through her slowly; she'd spent nearly every night here since coming to the Winter Court. This was a dream.

But even in her first dream, the cottage had felt familiar. As far as she could remember, she had never seen anything quite like it in the real world, but if she had to make a home for herself—outside of the one she shared with her family—this was the sort of home she would have chosen. It was perfect for quiet days alone, embroidering or reading, or entertaining a guest or two.

At that thought, a knock came at the door. She blinked and looked down at the tray in her hands.

Two steaming teacups sat on it. But hadn't she just poured the water in the kettle? She gave her head a small shake and set the tray on the table to answer the door.

It was the silvery fae, of course. He'd come to visit once before. At least, she thought he had. Trying to recall her other dreams was a hazy effort. But he seemed familiar; surely she'd seen him before.

As he had last time, he looked unnaturally attractive, with his broad shoulders and long silver hair. He carried himself with a proud, regal air that somehow also felt deeply dangerous—not as if she was in danger *from* him, but that anything that threatened her would suffer greatly. He was a man who knew how to protect and to rule, a fact doubly evidenced by the small silver circlet that rested on his brow. He was dressed in the exact same exquisitely made, soft silver tunic he'd had on last time. She bit her lip at the thought. In her waking hours, she couldn't remember what he looked like, save for the silver hair and blue eyes. How did she know that he wore the same clothes now?

"Won't you let me in?" His voice rumbled over her skin, scattering her thoughts like dust on a breeze.

"Of... of course." She stepped aside for him. He strode in and took a seat, not waiting for her to invite him to pick up one of the teacups. He held it to his nose and drew in a deep breath. When he glanced at her, his eyes were half-lidded in a way that sent a shiver through her body.

"I hope you like it." She hurried to drop into the seat across from him. "If you're going to keep up these visits, you should tell me what sorts of teas you prefer so that I can prepare those for you instead."

Something glinted in his face at that—wary amusement, or perhaps surprised delight. "Why are you so kind to me?"

She paused, her own cup halfway to her mouth. "Why wouldn't I be?"

"It's just..." He shook his head. "I'm not used to being treated with any sort of tenderness."

She took a sip of her tea to gather her thoughts. "In the waking world—" she began, but hesitated. Hadn't he left when she started prodding before? He was clearly fae, like the beast and Zoya. So perhaps, like them, he had to take care with his words. There was something at work in the Winter Court, something even Zoya, in all her kindness toward Kienna, refused to speak of. She continued, picking through her words. "Do you also live at the Winter Castle?"

The look in his glowing blue eyes was unreadable. It felt like a victory when he gave her a small nod.

She smiled, but the smile melted into a frown. "I've been there for weeks. Here," she corrected. Just because this place didn't look like the Winter Court's castle didn't mean she had escaped. "How have I never seen you?"

His eyes tightened, and he looked away. His long silvery hair slid over his chest as he did so. Her fingers twitched toward him, aching to know if it felt as silky as it looked.

"What do you think of the Prince of Winter?" he asked, his mouth curling into a small sneer at the name.

Kienna searched for words again, this time because she wasn't sure how to answer the question. "He hasn't hurt me. He's terrifying..." Admitting that to someone was like opening a window into her soul. A breath of fresh air, but the words made her guest's shoulders tense. She hurried on. "But as terrifying as he is, he *has* kept his word. I do... I do feel safe, for the most part. Perhaps it won't be so terrible, the rest of my year here. I only have to stay that long before I can return home to my family." A weight grew on her chest at the mention of them.

His chin dipped down against his chest.

Kienna tilted her head and studied him. The posture was almost one of defeat. "What do you think of the beast?" Tension rippled through him, sparking concern in her. "Has he hurt you?"

His laugh was bitter. "The beast has hurt everyone in the Winter Court, and he will only continue to do so."

She leaned back at the ferocity of his tone. "But your anger toward him seems personal," she murmured. "He's done something to you directly, hasn't he?"

The silence stretched. The longer it did, the more it felt like confirmation of her words.

"Cinnamon," he said abruptly. "I used to like cinnamon ginger tea."

She blinked at the unexpected shift and then smiled as a warmth suffused her. Just as suddenly as he'd spoken, the fae man stood. He towered over her, his presence demanding every bit of her attention. When he spoke again, his tone had shifted from quiet uncertainty to something more urgent. "Remember my words from before."

She stood too, a boldness lifting her hand to skim against the feathery ends of his hair; the back of her hand brushed against his tunic and the hard muscle beneath as the pads of her fingers curled in the silvery strands. If anything, it was softer than she had imagined. As silky and smooth as any of the wondrous fae fabrics in the waking world.

"Not to trust my eyes." She dared to look up at him. "What, then, should I trust?"

He was frozen under her touch, his eyes wide, his nostrils flared. He looked terrified.

She started to draw her hand away. Had she broken some sort of fae custom?

But with reflexes faster than anything she had seen before coming to the fae realm, he captured it in his own. His hands were large, rough, calloused. The hands of a warrior. Warm in the best way.

Her mouth went dry. She cautiously looked back up at him. His expression was one of agony. He searched her eyes, though she couldn't imagine what he was looking for. His grip on her tightened infinitesimally, and his eyes slid shut.

"Trust *me*." His words slid out in a rough, whispered plea.

"But how do I find you in the waking world?"

She might as well have bitten him for how he jerked away from her. "It doesn't matter."

And then he was gone—the door swinging shut behind him, Kienna's hand outstretched where he had left her. She pressed it into her stomach.

It did matter. She was absolutely certain of that. If she found him in the waking world, she suspected many of her questions about the Winter Court would be answered, because mysteries clung like a cloak to that man—that prince? He felt like a prince, with his regal air and subtle crown. He seemed like some sort of prisoner of the beast, given his reaction to him. Perhaps he was the rightful ruler of the Winter Court, and the beast had stolen the throne from him. It might explain the deplorable state of the Court.

Asking the beast about him would probably only make her task that much harder. No. She would keep her questions to herself and find the prince on her own.

CHAPTER 13
ENLO

Enlo was sitting in the small study down the hall from his personal suite when he heard the footsteps. His gaze snapped to the door. Most Elyri were so graceful and light-footed you hardly heard them coming, which could only mean...

The door, already slightly ajar out of his habit, creaked open as a golden head peeked through.

Kienna.

Enlo suppressed the grin that wanted to stretch across his face. He had kept his promise to Revi and not sought out Kienna. But if she came to find him—well, he could hardly be at fault for that.

She stared at him, eyes wide, taking in his face, his silver hair, his pointed ears. She lingered last on his eyes, her brow furrowing slightly, but after a moment she shook her head. She stepped into the room and shut the door behind her.

"I found you at last." She gave a hesitant smile.

Enlo's brows rose. She had been searching for *him*? Well, that made no sense, given she didn't even know he existed, but he wasn't going to let the opportunity slip him by on such a triviality.

He rose languidly and smiled at her with all the charm that he possessed. "Here I am."

She blinked. "Your voice is very smooth." Her own voice was breathy as she said it, but there was a note to it that made him pause.

"Is that a bad thing?" he asked, giving her his best, most charming quizzical look.

She bit her lip. "No. It's... it's very nice. Just not what I expected."

What she expected? Ever more curious.

"I'm afraid"—he sauntered closer to her—"I can't *always* live up to expectations."

Her breath caught as he paused a step away from her.

He tilted his head and gave her another lazy smile. "Are there any other expectations you had of me that I don't live up to?"

"I... I..." She stumbled over her words, a blush rising prettily to her face. He wanted to laugh. Weeks Revi'd had with her, and she hadn't even been in the same room as Enlo for five minutes before she was blushing.

She took a small step away as she gathered her courage and her words. "I wasn't expecting to find you in a study."

"No?" Enlo asked. "Where did you expect to find me?"

She looked around the room. "A dungeon. Somewhere less pleasant, at least. Imprisoned somehow."

Enlo let slip a surprised, bitter chuckle. "You don't have to be grimy and behind metal bars to be imprisoned, sweet flower."

She recoiled. "Don't." She drew herself straight, less sharp but no less firm. "Please don't call me that."

Enlo's brows rose. "Call you sweet, or a flower?"

"Either." She looked away as pain flashed across her expression.

Interesting. She wasn't a woman who wanted pretty pet names. Or him getting too close into her space, going by how she'd moved away. He filed both details away.

"You're right," she said softly. "Beautiful things can trap you too."

Enlo gave a hum of agreement, too busy studying her to formulate a worded response. She wore a summer dress today, just like she did most days now, this one in a soft green that complimented her eyes. It would be impossible to miss the sadness that lingered there.

"Kienna," he said, drawing her gaze back up to him and smiling with all the charm he possessed. "Are you happy here?"

She frowned at the question. "How—"

"Kienna?" a voice called, distant. Zoya.

He reached for Kienna's hands, testing the waters. "You must go. Come find me again soon. I spend much of my time here."

Her eyes widened, and she nodded.

"And you must swear not to tell anyone of this. If the beast were to learn that you had spoken with me..." He trailed off, letting her mind provide any implications.

Fear flickered in her gaze. "I promise."

He shook his head. "No, you must swear it in the way of the Elyri. *Tyshin dereht.* Say it with your name at the beginning."

"*Kienna tyshin dereht,*" she repeated, only slightly stumbling over the pronunciation. Her practice had served her well. A tinge of magic tugged from Enlo as it wrapped around her, sealing her vow.

Zoya called again, making Kienna's head whip around toward the door.

"Stay here," Enlo murmured. "I will send her away and give you time to slip back to your room."

He brushed past her and stepped out of the study. At the sight of him, Zoya dropped into a curtsy.

"My lord," she said in Elyri. "I'm sorry. I was just looking for Lady Kienna."

"This is hardly where she tends to spend her time," he said, giving Zoya a melting smile. "Have you checked the garden?"

"Yes... but I can check again."

"Perhaps she wandered from her usual routes," he suggested. "She doesn't go near the frostroses, does she?"

Zoya's eyes widened. "Not usually."

"Good. If the prince found her there, there's no telling what he would do."

Panic flooded through Zoya's expression. "I'll go check." She gave another curtsy, then turned and hurried away.

Enlo smirked. He returned to the study. Kienna waited right where he had left her, shifting from foot to foot.

"It's safe now." He stopped beside her, offering her a conspiratorial smile. "Hurry back to your room. I've sent her off to the garden."

"Thank you."

"You'll return soon, won't you? The days are long and lonely in this place."

"I will come back soon." She gave him a hesitant smile even as she searched his face. "I'm glad I found you."

Enlo couldn't resist the grin that slid over his face. "As am I."

CHAPTER 14
REVI

R evi waited in his frostcat form in the dining hall for Kienna to come. The servants had brought the food, warm under domed silver covers, and then left again, as usual.

There was only Revi and his thoughts. Even after all these weeks, the room still felt strangely empty without Enlo around. Not for the first time, a prickle of guilt trickled through Revi at his order for Enlo to keep away.

It had been the right decision. And, another part of him quietly admitted, now that he had seen how Kienna could smile, he found he wanted to share her with his cousin even less than before. His last visit to her dream echoed in his mind. The light brush of her fingers against his chest still burned through him. The way she had looked up at him...

If he could only see that look again. It made him believe that maybe love was possible, as fanciful as the idea was. Maybe it wouldn't be so terrible to break the curse by marrying Kienna. He admired her already, from her bravery to her kindness. That wasn't the same as *her* admiring *him*, but it was something.

And really, how hard could it be to be pleasant, to court her? He had done so before. Not courting, of course, but pleasantries. Before the curse, before his parents' disappearance... He had made nice with courtiers. Not as well as Enlo, but he had managed. He'd had a hold on the beast once before. He could do it again.

His resolve thus strengthened, he settled his head on his paws and waited.

And waited.

Time trickled away, and still there was no sign of Kienna. Irritation at her tardiness built minute by minute.

But no. She did not seem the sort to be late for no reason.

That thought washed away the irritation with a wave of concern. He'd gone to the library in the afternoon, but she'd been absent there as well. He hadn't thought too much of it. She didn't visit the library *every* day. But now, with her current absence... Had something happened to her? But surely if something had, he would have been notified. Unless...

He pushed himself to his feet and leaped down from the sofa. It couldn't hurt to just go check, to ensure that all was well. He was halfway across the room when the doors opened and Kienna stepped in, her cheeks flushed a rosy hue and her breath slightly ragged as if she had hurried.

He stopped abruptly. "My lady."

Kienna's gaze landed on him, and she dropped into a curtsy, her expression falling into a careful mask. "I apologize for my tardiness."

"It's no matter." He drew in a deep breath, nostrils flaring as he checked the air. There was no scent of blood. No sign of injury. Still, something seemed off. Kienna stood before him, quietly agitated. He had not seen her so since her first week here.

"Are you all right?" he asked, the question feeling awkward.

"Of course." The smile she gave him was stiff—cold, even. An edge of sweat tinged her scent. Her pulse moved a tick faster.

Was she... *lying* to him?

"Did something happen?"

Her pulse jumped again. "Of course not. What would give you that idea?" She brushed past him, skirting him by several paces. She took her seat with a stiff posture. "I'm famished."

He turned and padded after her, tail twitching behind him. Despite her protests, there was clearly something wrong. And Revi did not appreciate being lied to. It was a strange sensation, one he had rarely experienced in his life. He didn't want it to become familiar now.

Kienna plucked the domes off their plates and started eating with gusto.

"Did you..." Revi said haltingly, taking his own place but not touching his meat. It had gone cold, and he found he disliked the idea of cold cooked meat even less than the idea of it warm. "What did you do today?"

At the question, Kienna stiffened. Her fingers tightened imperceptibly on her fork before she stabbed it into a roasted vegetable. She didn't look at Revi. "I went exploring a bit. I found an art studio."

"Do you enjoy art?"

"Not particularly." Her voice was oddly short.

Was she angry with him? Was that why she was lying? Revi's claws pricked the fabric of the sofa before he forced himself to stop. Not every anger warranted a fight... and even if this anger did, he could not handle it with tooth and claw. He had a bargain to maintain. And beyond that, he found that even his usual predatorial instincts stayed quiet. He had no desire to harm her.

He thought over their recent interactions during the days, looking for any clue that would explain her strange behavior. Nothing came to mind. Their recent dinners had mostly been quiet. Their times in the library equally so as she read and he pretended to read but mostly enjoyed their companionable silence and listened to Kienna mutter as she studied his language—even helping her occasionally when she asked. It was good that Enlo didn't spend time with them in the library, or he would have teased Revi mercilessly for his obvious fascination.

But no. He could think of nothing that would warrant her ire, and yet here she sat, irritated, perhaps even angry, about something.

"What is wrong with you tonight?" He had no desire to dance around the subject or her feelings. Getting it out into the open was far more efficient.

That question earned him a look; her eyes widened with shock, then narrowed in that strange, unexplainable anger. "Why do you keep me here? Do you enjoy imprisoning people? Is this some sort of twisted game to you?"

"Your father took my rose—"

"I know that," she snapped, cutting him off.

He blinked, for a moment too frozen to react. He would have thought her too afraid of him to dare snap, but she had begun her tirade and there was no stopping her now.

"Why trap me?" she asked. "Why claim me for a year *and a day* if you're only going to send me back again? What purpose does it serve?" She threw a hand up toward the door. "Why—?" Her words cut off, and she froze, seeming like she was choking. She recovered herself with a large gulp from her water glass and crossed her arms. "I just want to understand. Zoya speaks highly of you when she dares to speak of you at all. You haven't been cruel, and yet you keep u—me here. What benefit do you get from trapping people in your dying Court?"

With every word she spoke, Revi's hackles raised. "I told you not to ask questions," he growled.

"If you would provide more answers, I wouldn't have to! Is it so terrible that I want to understand you? Understand this strange place that I have to call home for the rest of my year?"

"Perhaps you'll just have to trust me."

When he'd said that in the dream, she'd looked at him with affection, maybe even agreement. Now, she scoffed and crossed her arms. "Perhaps you should give me a reason to."

He rose to a crouch, claws digging deeper into the sofa. Everything in him wanted to pounce at her, to fight in the only way he knew how. It would be so easy. She was so weak, this human.

No.

As she stared at him, a fiery light in her eyes, he pushed back against the dark, monstrous urgings in his mind. No, she might not be as physically strong as he was, but this woman was not weak.

Instead, he leaped from the sofa and started pacing in front of the window. He kept his breath shallow, doing his best not to pull in the scent of her, which only made his bestial instincts flare.

"Why is it so hard to answer my questions?" she asked. "Are you under some sort of magic?"

He huffed out a breath. No, his curse had no magic that forbade him to speak of it, but he was also certain that telling her of it would not make it any more likely to be fulfilled. If anything, knowing the expectations of the curse would only frighten her, push her away further. What woman would want to know that she was expected to marry a beast she hardly even tolerated? Still, a part of him found himself wanting to give her something. But what could he possibly give her that would satisfy her?

He hadn't found the right words when she sighed. The motion deflated her, her anger trickling away to something closer to weariness.

"I don't know why I bother," she murmured, low enough that Revi was certain the words weren't meant for him. "Never mind," she said, raising her voice. "Come eat."

He turned to look at her fully. She was twisted halfway around in her seat and gave him a taut smile that didn't quite reach her eyes.

"I didn't mean to derail our dinner. I'm sorry for asking pointless questions."

He slinked closer warily, but her expression didn't shift back into anger, so he returned to his seat.

She picked up her fork again and took a bite of food. "If you're unwilling to answer those questions," she said after a moment, "perhaps you would answer another one for me?"

He stared at her, waiting. She chewed her lip.

"Where are the king and queen? You seem like the highest authority here, but the title 'prince' is not usually the highest authority."

A pang of loss shot through him at her words. Something must have showed in his demeanor, because she hurried to add, "If this is related to everything else you won't tell me, I understand. I've just been wondering."

"I don't know," he said quietly. "I don't know where my parents are." Her face softened at his admission, but he continued. This, at least, he could give her, as painful as it was for him. "It has nothing to do with your other questions. They vanished years ago; no one knows where to. They went out riding one day, and they never returned."

Her hand raised to cover her mouth. "I'm so sorry," she whispered through her fingers. "Were you close with them?"

The innocent query twisted through him. "Yes. And no. Their roles didn't always allow for the closeness I wanted. But I would have done anything for them, happily. I still would."

"You sound like you love them deeply."

He nodded. No words would ever properly convey the depth of his love.

Of his concern for them, even now.

"But if it's been that long," she continued, "why haven't you ascended the throne, taken the role of king?"

He grimaced. "Because they're not dead." Her brow furrowed, and he could already feel the question that was coming, so he answered it before she could ask. "If they were dead, their pine and moss would have withered with everything else. I would have the full power of the Winter Court at my command. Most of that power is my father's, but if he perished, it would fall to my mother. Only if both of them were gone would it transfer to me. I am the most powerful Winter Elyri here, and as a member of the royal family, that leaves me with the designation of the Heart of Winter, just like"—he cut himself out before mentioning Enlo's name—"just as anyone else with my blood would have. So I rule in their absence, but I am not the Winter King, and I will not become the Winter King until my parents have both perished."

She took all this in with wide eyes. "Have you ever tried to find them?"

He scoffed. "I have sent hundreds of men and women in search of them, but wherever they are, they left no tracks, no clues to follow. Either they do not want to be found"—he pushed away the familiar anger, the betrayal at the idea—"or someone else doesn't want them to be found."

The silence weighed heavy with his words. He felt exposed. He'd admitted one of his greatest pains to her. Dread tried to crowd his mind—he'd given her a way to hurt him; if she chose to, she could wield it against him. He had to protect himself, do something to keep her from using it to wound him—

"My mother died only a few years ago." A heavy weight of familiar sorrow filled her voice. It dragged the dread in his thoughts to a halt. "Brigands along the road when she was visiting a close friend who lived a few days from our home."

Revi tensed, instantly wanting to find these brigands and punish them. "Were they ever caught?"

"My father hunted for a year before he found them. It's part of why he was given his position; he became quite familiar with the Makarian countryside and people in the process." Kienna tucked her hair behind her ear. "But there was this terrible period, a span of a week when her carriage was first found and she wasn't. A week when we knew something horrible had happened, but we didn't know *what*. I was sick with worry and trapped at home. Powerless to do anything. I had only my hope, and it shredded a little more each day."

He knew the feeling well; he'd lived with it so long it felt an ingrained part of him, even more than his curse did. It made him want to go to Kienna, curl around her and protect her from it, even if only the memory of it.

He cleared his throat. "How did you finally find her?"

"They dumped her body along the road near where the carriage had been. I think they took her because they thought to ransom her, but she'd been injured in the initial attack. It was the infection that actually took her from us."

A deep growl escaped him. If anyone had ever dared do that to *his* mother—

He forced the thought away, focusing instead on the woman before him. "I'm sorry. That must have been shattering."

"It was. Like you, I would have done anything for her." She took in a shaky breath but tilted her face to smile at him. "It was the worst feeling I've ever experienced. But I remember that time of not knowing with a great deal of pain, too. It was only the hope of her return that brought me through it, until we found—" She cut off, squeezing her eyes shut for just a moment. "But you *know*. You know they're alive. And if they're alive, there's still hope to find them. Cling to that hope. It will see you through, too."

What a brave, strong woman she was. Baring what had to be one of the most horrible, painful moments of her life to him, only to *encourage* him. He'd never met anyone so incredibly unflinching before.

"I will," he promised, desperate for something to say. It felt inadequate, after her story, but he wanted to give her something in return. "I will never give up on finding them."

She nodded, seeming satisfied.

Silence wrapped around them. She picked at her food, but he just sat, wanting nothing more than to study her, understand her. He was searching for something to steer the conversation back to life when she spoke first.

"Is it difficult ruling when you aren't technically the final authority in your Court?"

He turned his head away from her, tensing. That was so far from a subject he wanted to explore with her. "I learned ways to discourage questions and doubt."

He didn't want to see what the admission would mean to her, how she would interpret it. Having to rule had probably been the true beginning of his descent into the beast he was now, but he couldn't afford to regret that, because he had used it first to secure his Court and later to protect it from outside threats.

Soft fingers sank into the fur at his shoulder. He froze, slowly turning back to look at her.

Kienna's expression was sorrowful. "I'm so sorry. That must have been such a difficult time."

"Luckily for me, I have always been good at monstrous things, even bef—" He cut himself off and stiffened. He'd almost admitted the curse to her in full. What was it about this woman that made him want to bare every corner of himself to her?

She was silent a long moment; he waited for her to question his slip, but when she spoke again, she sounded almost frustrated. "You aren't a beast just because you look like one."

"I am—and have been—a beast inside and out for years." The curse just better reflected his true nature.

"Maybe if you acted like one, yes." Her gaze drilled into him, as if she could will him to believe her. "If you were cruel, manipulative, vicious. But just having fangs and claws doesn't make you a monster. You are more than what you look like. You are who you *choose* to be. And you do what you must to rule your Court. Protecting people, especially at risk to yourself, is the opposite of monstrous."

He forced himself to relax under her touch, even as his entire being wanted to tense at her words. She'd reached out to him, and her fingers rested, still and small. He didn't want to frighten her away.

She was so delicate. He had no doubt that in many ways, she was the strongest of her kind, just not in the ways he had ever thought mattered before now.

But here she was, showing kindness to a beast, and it lit within him a cool whisper of hope. If she could be compassionate toward him, perhaps she could be more. If she could be more, perhaps it wasn't so foolish to think that *he* could change his nature and be more too, like she seemed to believe he could be.

It felt like an impossible dream.

It was a dream he wanted anyway. But first, he needed to rid his Court of the curse, or he'd have no time to find out.

"I choose to be who I must for my Court," he finally said, falling back on a familiar answer. "I'm the only one who can fulfill my role."

Kienna's fingers tightened slightly on his fur. "Aren't you... lonely?"

He considered the question. He'd never had many friends. Just Enlo, really. And now he had her, even if only by dint of trapping her here with a bargain. But that felt too exposing to say. "I am no lonelier than I've ever been."

She made a humming noise.

He tilted his head to better study her. "Are you lonely? Do you... miss your family? Your father?"

"Not lonely. But yes, I miss him." Her free hand moved to her chest as if she could hold in the ache she hid. The motion opened a similar ache in Revi's chest. If she felt that pain, it was entirely his doing.

A sharp thought occurred to him that made him want to raise his hackles. "Did you have anyone besides your family?"

Was her heart already claimed?

A small smile flickered with her usual brilliance even as it knifed at Revi's heart. "Yes, but not what you might expect." She laughed at his bemusement. "I kept rabbits."

Revi blinked. The jealousy washed away, only to be replaced by sheepishness. "Rabbits?"

She laughed outright. "For their fur. Well, originally. My mother loved the feel of rabbit fur specifically, so I got them to spin the fiber to make her things. But they're just lovely creatures. Soft and cuddly and sweet. I go—" She cut off. "I mean, I used to go to their hutches every day to care for them—feed them, comb their fur to collect the fiber, things like that. They were all fairly friendly, but one of them, my favorite—I named her Mushroom. She's the fluffiest, a lovely silvery grey, and she'd always hop to the door of their enclosure to greet me when I came and bury her nose in the crook of my neck." Her hand went to her neck absently as she spoke, a melancholic shadow cast over her features.

Revi swallowed. He'd never been so irrationally jealous of a prey animal before.

"And ever since she died, I find they remind me of her." Her shoulders drew in, and he could hear her swallow, even as her eyes glistened.

She drew her hand back from his coat and stood. "I find I don't have much appetite tonight."

Revi rose quickly, bumping into the table. He wasn't ready for her to leave. "Would you like to walk to the kitchens with me? I smelled some sort of pastry baking earlier." A lemon cake with vanilla. It sounded completely unappealing to him, but perhaps Kienna liked sour-sweet.

"Oh, no, thank you." She gave him a small curtsy. She tried to mask the melancholy in her mien with a smile, but it didn't reach her eyes. "Good night."

"Kienna, wait—"

She ignored him. Her steps made a shuffling whoosh on the stone floor as she hurried from the room, but the sound couldn't hide her soft sniffling.

Revi wanted to rip his teeth into something. He wanted to comfort her, yet she fled. Because why would she want comfort from *him*? She was mourning the loss of her home, her family, her beloved pets, and it was *his* fault.

He was the worst kind of monster—no matter what she said to the contrary.

CHAPTER 15
ENLO

E nlo curled his hand into a fist, pulling himself back from the magic he'd used to watch Revi and Kienna. Logically, he knew he should be glad Revi seemed to have made some progress with Kienna on his own—if reminding her of what she'd left behind could truly be called *progress*—but he couldn't pretend that the dark feeling curling through him was relief. It probably wouldn't last. They'd come to some sort of temporary camaraderie tonight—but only because Kienna had chosen to drop the subject of prisoners.

But Revi had already pushed her away again by the end of the meal. She'd left crying. It changed nothing, and Enlo would still have to fix the mess himself. Which would be much easier if Kienna would come find him again during the day. He could only hope she would.

A sharp thump came at his door. Enlo froze before striding to open it. Revi didn't wait for an invitation before pushing past Enlo into the room, his huge frostcat form filling the space.

Enlo resisted slamming the door behind him. The click of the latch was lost in Revi's next words.

"I need your help," he said without preamble.

Enlo's brows climbed. "My help with...?" He let the question trail, even though he suspected he knew exactly what Revi wanted his help with.

"How do you..." Revi was pacing, his tail lashing, his manner overtaken by agitation, though he did not seem angry, precisely. "How do you make women happy?"

Enlo glided to his armchair near the empty fireplace. "It doesn't take much, really. All I have to do is smile at them."

A low growl rolled up Revi's throat. "That's not helpful, Enlo. I smile"—he paused to give an example, baring his fangs—"and people quake in fear. Not express joy."

"It's good to see you taking your endeavor a little more seriously. I assume that's what this is about?"

Revi grunted. "Sure. What would you do to... win the heart of a lady?"

Enlo shrugged. "I would make her feel special, wanted, desired. I would lavish her with attention and gifts, make her feel as if I truly saw her. Remember small important details about her and use them to my advantage later. It's like a hunt, but instead of chasing down the prey, I'm luring her in, drawing her willingly to me." He smirked at Revi. "Of course, this is all made easier by the fact that I am irresistible." He gestured a lazy hand toward himself. "I'm afraid I have no real advice for someone whose preferred meal is rare and bloody."

Revi huffed. He rubbed his nose against one paw. "I only know one way of hunting, and that would definitely violate our bargain."

Enlo leaned forward, resting his elbows on his knees. "I want to help you, cousin. Of course I do. But I am at as much of a loss as you are on how to be a charming beast. No one finds the monsters charming.

Women may coo over cute animals, but that's hardly helpful in your case."

Revi's tail stilled. "Maybe it could be," he said slowly.

Enlo chuckled. "Have you ever seen a baby animal? You look nothing like one. No, I think your best chance is to just be patient and courteous. And take care not to scare the woman, and hope that with time she warms to you. Time is your friend here. You have months left. A lot can happen in that time."

Revi gave Enlo a distracted frown. "I thought you were the one who said we were running out of time."

"Then make the time we have count." Enlo forced a smile. "Use it wisely."

"Will even a year be long enough for someone to fall in love with a beast?" Revi said drily.

"We can only hope," Enlo said. It would be more than enough time for someone to fall in love with *him*. He just needed his cousin not to frighten her away in the meantime.

CHAPTER 16
REVI

By the time Revi arrived at the dining room the next day, he could already hear the soft movements of Kienna within.

It had taken him far longer to move through the halls in this form, but he'd wanted to practice moving so he wouldn't make a complete fool of himself. He could only hope his efforts would be worth the trouble.

The door creaked as he entered.

"Good evening...?" Kienna's voice ended in a question, and her chair scraped back. It took all of Revi's self-control not to flee from the room. He was no coward. If she laughed at him... Well, it would be more than he had managed to evoke from her thus far during the day.

He took a deep breath and kept moving. He avoided looking at himself in the dark window lining the wall. He was doing this for her, but if he saw his own reflection, in *this* form, there was a good likelihood he wouldn't keep moving.

Footsteps sounded. "Hello? Beast? Zoya?" Kienna neared and froze. Revi quashed down his prey instincts—a side effect of the form he hadn't expected and was *not at all* fond of.

He inclined his head with as much dignity as he could manage. "Good evening, Lady Kienna."

"You're..." Kienna took in his small form with wide eyes.

He twitched his nose and shifted.

"You're a rabbit," she said faintly.

"You seemed melancholic after our last dinner," Revi said, looking just past her shoulder. He couldn't meet her eyes—he couldn't bear to see the laughter, to see if there was mockery as she observed him. "I thought perhaps this form would be more soothing to you than my regular choices."

"Oh," she whispered. She sank to the ground slowly, her skirt puddling around her.

Revi was at a loss. She hadn't laughed at him, but neither did she look happy.

"If you don't like it—"

"No, it's..." She cleared her throat. "It was very thoughtful. I'm sorry, I... I was aware you could change forms, since I've seen you as both a wolf and a frostcat, but I just... I never expected to see you looking quite like this."

"It's not my usual choice," Revi said stiffly.

"You look..." She trailed off again.

"Ridiculous."

"No," she said quickly. "No, not at all, you..."

He glanced over at the window running the length of the room beside them. He was a rabbit. Not the smallest rabbit he had ever seen, but a rabbit nonetheless. With silver fur and long ears that flopped slightly. Despite what she said, he *definitely* looked ridiculous.

Quiet sniffling drew his gaze back to her. Horror flooded him—tears tracked down her cheeks.

"I'm sorry," she said as he took a half step forward. She pulled her skirt up to dab at her face. "I'm sorry. It's just..." She turned away.

"It does not please you."

"It's not that. Th-thank you for this. It's incredibly thoughtful." She gave him a watery, wavering smile. "I just—I miss—" She shook her head abruptly and swallowed the words back. "May I... may I pet you?"

He jerked back at the request but recovered quickly. "I... suppose," he agreed gruffly. He'd done this for her. If he was going to debase himself as if he were a pet, he might as well submit to the full treatment.

She reached out a hand, and he closed the distance until her fingers curled through his fur in a slow, rhythmic motion. Her hand covered a good portion of his side, and only an iron will kept him from retreating. She was so much *larger* than him. He was unused to being the smallest creature in the room. Shorter, by dint of four-legged versus two-legged anatomy, but his regular forms were equal—or even larger—than a person as far as general size was concerned. But rabbits were tiny. Squashable, really.

"You look so—very much—" Her words stumbled and halted again, her grip tightening slightly against his side before she resumed her stroking. It was... incredibly comfortable. He resisted the urge to lean into her touch, but he couldn't keep his nose from twitching with his delight.

"You make an excellent rabbit," she finally finished. It was clear that was not at all what she'd been about to say.

"I know perhaps it's not quite the same as the rabbits you had at home." He kneaded his paws into the floor. He was beyond ready to be done with this conversation. Not the petting, perhaps, but the speaking. The idea that it had seemed clever before felt utterly foolish. She probably thought he was mocking her and the story she'd trusted him with. How could he have thought that even in this form he could ever be soothing to her? "I've never seen one of your rabbits bred for fiber. I only know what the ones in the wild look like." Generally as they fled from him. Before he ate them.

His prey instincts made his heart pitter-patter at the thought.

Being a rabbit didn't suit him.

"It-it's all right," she said. "It's not like I would want to use your fur to spin anything anyway. Not that"—she blushed and stumbled over her words—"not that there's anything wrong with your fur. It's quite lovely; I just—"

"No," he agreed quickly. "That was never on offer."

She laughed, but the laugh quickly turned to a sob. Her fingers tightened again, almost painfully so.

Enough of this. Revi stepped back to put space between himself and Kienna.

"*Zeminy.*"

He gritted his teeth as his body stretched, grew—as familiar and agonizing as ever. Kienna was sobbing now, her face buried in her hands.

Back in his more familiar wolf form, Revi hesitantly padded forward and lowered himself to the ground, resting his head on her knee.

"I'm sorry." It was paltry, but it was all he had to offer her.

She dropped a hand and buried it in his fur, pulling so hard that it hurt. But he tensed himself and held still, ignoring the instincts to fight back against the one who caused him pain. Sobs racked her, and as her head slumped forward with each one, Revi pushed up into a sitting position so that he caught her head on his shoulder. He didn't know what else to do, but as she cried, he stayed there.

That, at least, he could do.

CHAPTER 17
KIENNA

T his time when Kienna woke up in her cozy cottage, her recollection that it was a dream came almost immediately, between one breath and the next.

She put water on for tea and sank into the chair next to the fire. The lights filling the space seemed drabber today, or the color of everything was flatter; her dream state reflected her melancholy.

She briefly considered trying to change the dream. She missed home terribly, especially after the past few conversations with the beast. *Especially* after that evening. That he had even thought to shift into a rabbit, something surely so against his instincts, just because she'd made a passing comment about missing home and her pets...

The thoughtfulness of it nearly overwhelmed her. She didn't know what to do with this version of the beast, one who wasn't so stoic and prideful.

And the way he'd appeared in the dining room, looking like an almost exact replica of Mushroom—his fur had been silky soft, just like hers.

Perhaps she could conjure up a replica of home here. But after considering the idea for a moment, she decided against it. It wouldn't be home just because it looked like it, just like this cottage wasn't home, despite how her mind tried to whisper to her that it was. She didn't want to see fake versions of her family. That would only dig the ache deeper.

A part of her wanted to wake up. Being alone in this dream cottage felt unappealing. If only her regular companion would appear with his silvery hair and glowing blue eyes. She much preferred her dreams with him than those without. She supposed she could have snuck away to find him in the waking world too, now that she knew *where* to find him. But he was just so... *much* in the waking world. He overwhelmed her with the way he didn't have the same reserved manner, how he'd crowded into her space with his touches and smiles. It should have been flattering, but instead it put her off-kilter. Maybe she just needed to go meet him again—she'd only visited him once. She needed to give it more time. He... he just felt like a different person.

Maybe he was. Maybe she'd found the wrong man.

The idea prickled along her spine. If he wasn't her dream prince, then who exactly had she found? And why had he let her believe she knew him?

She wouldn't avoid him in the waking world forever. She just needed to figure out how to suss out if he was who she thought, and if he wasn't... how to handle that.

And if he was her dream prince, she just wanted time to become accustomed to the idea of that loud, bright version of him. His presence in her dreams was calmer. Comforting and steady. She missed him when he wasn't here.

She shook her head. It wasn't logical to miss the prince. She didn't even know him—not the man she'd found in the waking world, nor the man in her dreams. All she truly knew was that her dream prince felt dangerous, but not to her. She didn't even know his name. But then, that was the way of the fae world she found herself in, wasn't it? It wasn't like she knew the name of anyone else here either, besides Zoya. Even the beast hadn't given his true name.

And the beast—he was another man of contradictions. Of all the people in the Winter Court, he was the one she felt she knew the best, and still she knew so *little* about him.

Perhaps at their next dinner, she would ask him more. After all, he had opened up to her about his parents, and he had comforted her this evening. He always seemed so proud, dignified. Every inch the prince he was, even in an animal form. But he had chosen a different form—for *her*. A form it had been clear he found uncomfortable. And she had shown her gratitude by weeping on him.

She pressed her hands to her flushing cheeks. That had not been her finest moment. She truly didn't know what to make of him. He was a mystery to her, one she found herself wanting to understand. She had to stay in this place for a full year; the least she could do was befriend her only companion.

Not her only companion, she corrected herself. She had her prince, her fellow prisoner, as well. The thought of him only served to further complicate the feelings in her chest toward the beast.

A knock at the door broke through her reverie. She jumped to her feet. The kettle over the fire was whistling as well. How had she not heard it?

She pulled it quickly off the fire and set it on the table on her way to the door. There he was, as tall, broad-shouldered, and intense as ever, but there was something different today. His long hair was pulled back, halfway done up in a braid that fell over his shoulder with the loose bottom half of his hair. Even with the change, he looked as much the prince as ever. His circlet crown glinted as he tilted his head.

Kienna smiled at him. "It's as if my thoughts summoned you."

He raised a delicate brow. "You were thinking of me?"

When he put it that way... She turned quickly to hide her blush from him. "Come in. I'm sorry the tea isn't quite ready yet. I was caught up in my thoughts."

"Of me." His voice was too serious to tell if he was teasing her or not.

She busied herself pouring the tea. "No, not at all. I..." She let out a slow sigh. "I was thinking of home." It was true enough. She had been thinking of home before her thoughts turned to the man before her and the beast. It was the safest thing to admit, anyway.

His mouth tightened. "You are homesick?"

"Yes," she admitted, her hands stilling. It was like him speaking the word allowed something in her to loosen, to grieve.

She *was* homesick.

The prince's eyes tightened. "I'm sorry."

She shrugged. If anyone could understand her desire to be free, it would be him, her fellow prisoner. "In general, it's lovely here, really. It... it just isn't home."

He shook his head. "What you've seen of the Winter Court in the waking world is a mockery of what it's supposed to be like. The Court I grew up in is so much more than this wasteland we have now. There was nearly always snow, and the cool crispness in the air was the perfect contrast to the pale winter sun. Everything glistened like jewels, and fires filled our hearths, giving us a place to warm ourselves, to gather together after a day spent in the cold." His voice, which had grown impassioned with his words, dropped. He curled his hands over the back of the chair he stood behind. "That was home."

His words resonated in her, calling forth memories of sled rides, of building snow angels and snowmen, of the perfect crystalline stillness in the forest in winter.

"I would have liked to see that," she said softly.

He cast a sideways glance at her. "If you truly mean that... I could show you."

She made a face at him, wrinkling her nose. "I do not say things I don't mean, good sir."

A flicker of a smile graced his face, and he held his hand out. "Come with me."

She didn't hesitate to put her hand in his. His fingers curled around hers, rough and warm and strong.

And then he was pulling her toward the doorway. He stopped on the threshold and glanced back at her. "Close your eyes."

She obeyed, pressing one eye shut at a time. The action earned her another quirk of a smile on his face before she could no longer see him. His fingers tightened on hers, and she could almost feel an exhale before he whispered a word in Elyri she hadn't learned yet and pulled her through the door.

A gust of cold air kissed her face, pushing her hair back with enough force that she gasped at the shock of it. Her eyes flew open.

Everywhere around them was glistening white. She spun in a circle. Her dream cottage was gone; instead, behind her stood the Winter Court castle, its roof covered in snow, with beautiful, proud evergreens guarding its perimeters. Around her, impossibly, was a garden in full bloom. Silvery flowers, blue flowers, light pink flowers edged in white, deep green bushes, and trees rustling with needles. She had never even seen most of these plants, but clearly they thrived amongst the snow and the ice and the frost that glittered on their leaves and petals.

"Come." The prince tugged her forward.

She let him pull her along as she drank in her surroundings. She no longer wore one of her summer dresses; she was cloaked in layers of wool, softer than anything she'd ever worn, with a simple, elegant wooden brooch clasping the outer cloak. They followed a path cleared of snow around the side of the castle. When they came to the back, he tugged her off the path, their boots crunching and leaving two sets of prints behind them as they went. It was the same path she and the beast had taken once before, near the beginning of her stay at the Court.

He wove between bushes until he came to one that she recognized in full, glorious bloom, though it looked different surrounded by vitality beyond its own. *This* flower she knew well: the frostrose her father had taken, the flower that had led to the bargain that had paused her life. The ones the beast had shown her that day in the gardens. Each of them was just as magical, silver, and glittering as they'd been when she'd seen them that day.

He slowed there but didn't stop, the fingers of his other hand brushing against one of the roses even as he continued onward. The ground started to slope down, and finally they reached her companion's destination: a pond entirely frozen over.

Kienna hesitated even as the prince continued forward. At the resistance, he stopped and looked back at her.

"Is that safe to walk on?" She tried to keep her voice light but failed entirely. Her gaze flicked back and forth over the ice.

"Of course." His eyes softened. "Even if this were not a dream, I would ensure that it would be no threat to you." He squeezed her hand and gently tugged it, not demanding but inviting. "Trust me. I'll protect you."

Kienna stared out at the blue-white ice covering the small pond. She had heard of ice skating, but she had never done it herself. The idea of the ice breaking and being swallowed into the freezing water below *terrified* her. She took a step forward, and then another, until her side brushed her companion's.

He squeezed her hand again and moved forward, wrapping his other arm around her shoulders and pressing her against his side as they moved.

It felt good there. Safe.

On the next step, she looked down and realized she was wearing skates with a blade along the bottom of each sole. Her grip on her prince tightened.

"I've got you." He squeezed her shoulder. "Move like this." He pushed one leg out, and then the other, showing her how to glide across the ice. Where he was sure-footed, she wobbled, but he was patient and sturdy, keeping her from falling as they moved together.

After a while, he released his grip on her shoulder and held her elbow and hand instead. She immediately missed the comforting weight of his arm around her, but he kept murmuring soothing words of encouragement, and the longer they skated, the more her confidence grew.

They circled the pond several times before coming to a slow stop where they had begun. Kienna was breathless. Her cheeks and nose stung from the cold, but a joy had built in her chest. A joy for this place. Of being with him.

She beamed at him. "That was marvelous."

He rumbled an agreement in his chest, the sound familiar somehow.

"Can we go again?"

"I'm afraid my magic is limited. I can't maintain this illusion for very long." His mouth twisted down in a grimace at the admission, and his words doused her joy.

She looked around, seeing her surroundings in a new light. Remembering what they looked like in the waking world. Dusty and brown and barren, despite the frequent night rains. Nothing at all like this vibrant winter wonderland.

"What happened here?" The question tore from her. She ached for the loss of this beauty nearly as much as she ached for her own home.

As she watched, everything around them faded away, and suddenly they were by her cottage again, the blistering sun beating down on their heads.

Her prince turned around and opened the door to her cottage, not meeting her gaze.

"The beast did."

CHAPTER 18
REVI

R evi raked his claws across the paper, shredding it into ribbons that fluttered to the floor.

He was so, *so* tired. He'd thought he had dealt with the *zruyeds*. He always thought he'd dealt with them, but they always kept coming back.

Pushing to his feet, he stalked from the room, tail lashing. Better to leave quickly and get it over with. His steward would tell Enlo where he'd gone. Kienna...

It was better if he didn't tell her. He needed to embrace his inner beast for this task, and she made him want to be... different. Better than a beast.

But he had to be a monster to fight monsters.

And he had to get there quickly. He considered his current form. Good for fighting and bursts of speed, but not his favorite for long treks. "*Zeminy.*"

A ripple of pain, and then he loped down the hall again, now a wolf. He'd run for days as a wolf. This form would get him to the *zruyeds* invading his lands.

He made it to the entry hall before he was intercepted.

"Beast?"

He tensed at the feminine voice and reluctantly looked over his shoulder.

Kienna stood at the foot of the stairs, as radiant as ever. "It's almost dinnertime. I was just headed to the dining hall. Are you..." Her eyes tracked over him, as if looking for some clues to his plans. "Are you leaving?"

"There have been reports." He kneaded his paws into the rug beneath him. "Enemies have breached the borders of my Court. I must go protect my people."

"Oh... When will you return?"

Did he imagine the concern in her voice? It was wishful thinking to consider that perhaps she might miss him.

He longed to cross the room and wrap his arms around her as he had in the dream. But he was not that man. He had claws, not hands, and today he had to go use those claws to be the beast his Court needed him to be. To protect their borders. No matter how weary he was of the fighting. He was the Winter Prince, and protection fell, first and foremost, to him. He had warriors he commanded, but they had to stay stationed where they were, at the border itself. If *zruyeds* had slipped by them, those nuisances were his task.

"I don't know."

"I see." Kienna twisted her hands together. "Well... Be safe."

He blinked. He was never safe when hunting *zruyeds*, but the fact that she gave him such well wishes at all locked around his heart. He inclined his head to her. "I'll return when I can."

When the enemy was vanquished, he added mentally. When his Court was safe.

When *she* was safe.

CHAPTER 19
ENLO

E nlo didn't search out Kienna when Revi took leave of the castle. He'd promised, after all.

But his promise didn't constrain him from using his magic to send her a message, and if she chose to heed the invitation on it... Well. The promise said nothing of *her* seeking him out.

His lips curved into a smile as he heard the quiet, swift steps behind him. He schooled his expression into one more neutral and turned from the window he stood at, overlooking the pitifully low pond in the back garden. No matter how it rained, it never stayed full.

Kienna's eyes lit up at the sight of him, but there was an odd twist to her smile.

Enlo let his own smile widen as he drank her and her summer dress in. "You came."

"Of course," she said simply. "I was glad to get your note. After how you left so abruptly last time, I..."

Enlo tilted his head. "You took your leave of *me* last we met."

"No, not the library. From my cottage. After the skating."

Enlo blinked slowly, careful to keep his smile in place as he sifted through this. He'd watched her with his magic enough to know she had only her rooms in the castle. There were no cottages on the castle grounds.

Understanding clicked into place. Kienna's reaction last time he'd met her, in the library. Her expectations of what he'd be like.

It seemed Revi had been busy after all—during nights, at least.

Irritation tingled along Enlo's skin. Revi's attempts to woo the lady at the dinners were abominably poor, but what had he told her in the dreams? Surely not much, since she didn't know the prince from her dreams and the beast were one and the same.

Still, it rankled him that he didn't know what they were about while sleeping. Especially since she thought *Enlo* was the one she met.

Kienna still watched him, that small crease between her brows.

"My apologies. Dreamwalking stretches my skills." True. He could hardly manage it, not like Revi. He stepped closer to her—not so close as to push her boundaries like last time. Just close enough to indicate his interest. It was all a game, and no one played it better than him. Her skin flushed, but she didn't shift away. Good. He was still within her boundaries. "But I could never be angry with you, Kienna."

"O-of course," she stammered. "It must have been especially taxing to change everything for so long while we ice skated."

Enlo's brows flew up before he could stop them. Had Revi wasted precious magic to change her dream so thoroughly? It was one thing to insert himself into it. An entirely different thing to pull magic to change it. The Court *needed* that magic—far more than a human did.

Kienna's eyes darted between his, the tiny crease returning. Enlo mastered his expression and gave her an easy smile as the half-truth slipped past his lips. "You are well worth my efforts, I assure you."

"What did you want to do today?" she asked, searching his face as if looking for something.

Probably trying to understand the discrepancies she might remember between him and Revi. It could be difficult to recall details from dreams, but it could be done. Enlo would just have to distract her from the task.

"Anything, Kienna, as long as I'm with you. This place has a new life with you here. I could almost come to love the warmth of it, given how it suits you so well."

That earned him an askance glance. "You don't have to twist your words to flatter me. I remember too clearly what you said before about hating the husk of what your Court has become."

Enlo flinched. That was exactly how he truly felt, but he had never told her that.

Had Revi? The idea made him want to scoff. His cousin would never admit something so personal to anyone, much less the human he was so stiff with. His pride wouldn't allow such weakness to show.

"I only meant that you make it more bearable," he said smoothly, gliding to her side again. He gestured for the doorway. "Come, let's call for some tea. I'd love to read to you in the library." He had just the book in mind—something he knew she'd enjoy based on her choices when he'd observed her with his soulwalking.

Really, wooing women was so easy if you just paid attention to details. He didn't know how Revi was so terrible at it.

She followed him, her expression still somewhat guarded, but Enlo wouldn't let that bother him. He'd spend the day swaying her heart to him with some of the most romantic Elyri love stories he could find. She'd be back in the palm of his hand by nightfall. And then he'd start again tomorrow. And the next day. He would make the most of his cousin's absence to soak in this delectable challenge.

CHAPTER 20
REVI

R evi considered skirting the village. He wore his frostcat form so that he could crouch high up in a conifer and observe the ongoings, of which there were little. His people had all received messages to stay inside as much as possible until he had dealt with the threat. It made his hunting easier if there weren't bystanders that he had to worry about protecting. It was easier to keep them safe from the enemies—and from himself.

He shook the thought away. He would not hurt his people, even in the bloodlust of battle. Still, it was easier if they were inside when he passed by on his patrol.

It also meant Revi didn't have to speak to them. He would do anything to protect them, but he had never been the one for speaking. That was Enlo's purview.

Something, though, made him pause at this village. Something tugged on his senses. Despite how far from the Winter Castle he was, the sun beat down. The land felt parched. Dried up. Life struggled here even more so than the other border villages he'd passed recently. That, perhaps, was something Revi could help with, even if he could only give them a brief respite.

He made his way down from the tree, putting one paw silently in front of the other until he touched earth. He slunk forward, little more than a shadow moving in the shade of the trees. He didn't need to go into the village to do what he was going to do, but the closer he could get, the more it would help.

He stopped just on the edge of the forest and pressed his nose to the ground, letting his senses flood with the feel of the land here. The complete lack of magic. It was bereft, utterly devoid of any sense of Winter's magic.

His lips pulled back in a silent snarl, familiar hatred burning up for the woman who had cursed his home, and for himself. Always for himself. His vision tinged red, but he pushed away the anger. It would not serve him in his task.

He reached deep in his well of magic; the cool touch of it was a relief from the oppressive summer heat, even if the sensation of coolness was internal. He funneled the cold up through him and breathed it out along the earth. One breath. Another. Another.

With considerable effort, he cut the magic off and sagged against the earth. He had given so much and yet... it had barely done anything to this place. He could have been imagining the small dip in the temperature of the air. It wouldn't last. It wasn't enough. His people needed more, but the simple fact was that there was no more. The magic of the Winter Court was melting away a little more each day.

When he felt less shaky, he rose to his feet. He had done what he could for this small village. He had to resume his hunt. He couldn't return to the castle until he was certain the threat was resolved.

Not for the first time since he had left, his thoughts turned to Kienna. Of course she was fine while he was gone. He trusted Zoya to take care of her physical needs, and yet... He longed to see her, to be near her, so that he could be the one to help her if she needed anything.

The thought was ridiculous.

"My prince?" The voice that interrupted his thoughts was high and flutelike, like a small breeze on a winter morning.

He bristled and looked around. He had not heard anyone approach. That was an unforgivable mistake when *he* was supposed to be the hunter.

"It *is* you," the voice said again. A small figure stepped out from behind a tree. A boy, Revi realized. He was thin, with grey-white skin the color of birch bark and a gauntness to his cheeks that had less to do with his Elyri nature and more to do with the difficulty of growing food in the current climate.

His eyes were wide as he took in Revi. He dipped in a quick bow.

"I thought I felt... a pulse," he said, his voice hesitant and quivering. "A bit of heartbeat to the land. My ma said I was imagining it, but my senses have always been a bit more sensitive than others."

Revi looked away. He couldn't bear the fragile hope in this boy's expression.

"I did what I could," he said roughly. "It wasn't enough."

The boy's bright smile said otherwise. "The air already feels much better than it did before. Thank you, my prince."

"You shouldn't be outside," Revi growled. "I'm in the area because I am hunting."

The boy paled slightly. "I'm sorry. I just wanted a glimpse of you." His throat bobbed, and he raised a fist in a small burst of passion. "I know some people blame you for the curse, but Ma and I don't. If I was older, I'd go and wreak havoc on the Summer Queen for what she did to you. She deserves it!"

Revi blinked. "As... much as I appreciate the enthusiasm, that would defy my direct order to take no vengeance on her."

The boy flushed. "Right. Of course I wouldn't defy your command, my prince."

Giving that order had been difficult. He wanted nothing more than to rage against the Summer Queen, but he had no right to—he had wronged her when he'd claimed she'd broken their bargain with the few troops she'd sent.

He had broken the bargain, not she. He *was* the one to blame.

He couldn't bear to admit that to this boy, though. He didn't want to see that flame of admiration leave the boy's eyes—even if he deserved the scorn that would follow.

Revi shifted, desperate for a different topic. "Do you... does your village need anything else? I can send some supplies back from the castle when I return."

The question felt foolish. This boy was not the one to ask about that, and Revi's steward was surely in contact with the villages, but he had to offer *something*. What he had done so far was too paltry. It didn't measure up to the gleam of joy in this boy's eyes, to the loyalty he espoused toward Revi.

The boy shook his head violently. "Oh, no, my prince. We've got plenty. Well, not plenty, but we can manage with what we have. Freezing some Winter back into the place was more than enough. I—"

Something brushed against Revi's senses, and his hackles rose. He cut off the boy's rambling. "Get inside. Now."

The boy froze for half a second.

"*Now*," Revi snarled.

The boy vanished without another word. Revi spared him one last glance before he turned in the direction of the threat. In a leap, he was back in the tree, bounding across branches. The farther he could get from the village, the better.

The forest could have been dead for how quiet it had gone. No birds sang, no wind even stirred the branches.

He breathed deeply, picking out individual scents as he neared his prey. There were at least half a dozen, smelling of sulfur and rotten vegetation. He withheld the growl that rose in his chest.

How had six *zruyeds* gotten so close to a village without anyone noticing? He'd been to the border before this. His men there had seen the breach, but they'd thought it was *two*. Not six.

The answer came unbidden. He was the one who should have noticed, but his magic was too weak to stretch that far. Revi pushed away the claws of guilt sinking into his heart. He shifted to one last tree, and the beasts came into view. They looked like bears, though their bodies were lanky and thin. Their fur hung off them in greasy strings and their claws were blade-sharp and twice as long as a normal bear's. They prowled through the forest as if *they* were the hunters today. Revi bared his fangs. He would enjoy disabusing them of that notion. He dropped from the tree onto the back of one, claws extended in silent death.

The others were already moving toward him as he rose from the corpse of their fallen comrade. A base hunger flashed in all their eyes. They were little more than dumb beasts, but they were dumb beasts controlled by something else, and each of them harbored a savagery that would easily wipe out the more peaceful members of his Court.

Revi leaped forward. He didn't use magic in this fight. He had learned long ago that doing so would only aid his enemy as they sucked it from him to strengthen their own bodies.

No, this was a fight of monsters. In these moments, he was only a beast, like them. Teeth and claws, speed and death. He gave himself over almost entirely to his bloodthirsty instincts. He fell into the familiar dance, tearing apart his prey, dodging their poisonous claws and fangs. One by one, he took them down.

Until, at last, the clearing was still. He stood among the carnage, body shaking, aching for something else to fight.

The threat was over. He wrestled himself under control, repeating those words to himself. Slowly, normal sounds filtered back into the forest around him. Birds chirping, the distant rustling of woodland creatures.

When he felt mostly back to himself, he looked around the small battlefield. He had torn through the six *zruyeds*; his own body was covered in the evidence. He took a step forward and winced at the twinge in his side. He looked back. With all the blood on him, it took a moment to pinpoint the source.

It seemed he had not successfully avoided every attack like he had hoped. He grimaced, resisting the instinct to yelp at the pain as he continued forward. He didn't know if it was a bite or from the *zruyeds'* claws. One would almost certainly get infected and the other would leak venom throughout his body.

Either way, he needed to return home as quickly as possible.

CHAPTER 21
ENLO

Days passed, and Enlo spent every single one of them with Kienna.

She laughed with him, her eyes lighting up, but in the quiet moments when he would look over at her, sometimes he would catch her staring at him with her brow furrowed. And still she avoided any physical overtures from him whenever he tested to see if she was warming to his presence, his touch. It baffled him—and felt like a challenge. He'd never encountered a woman who didn't want to touch him. Perhaps it was her prudish human nature coming out. But he heeded her subtle clues, keeping to her boundaries so she'd stay comfortable. He'd settle with winning her heart from a distance if that was what it took. It was only a matter of time.

They spent their first few days in the library or a drawing room, reading or playing *vyna*—an Elyri strategy game Kienna mastered surprisingly quickly. He hadn't expected her human mind to be quite so keen.

But a week after Revi had left, Kienna's restlessness was making it remarkably hard for Enlo to concentrate.

He sighed at her quiet shifting for the dozenth time and pushed away from their game board. "You are not made for *vyna* today, I think."

She looked up at him, her expression somewhere between startled and guilty. "I'm sorry. I didn't mean to disturb you. I can return to my room."

"No," Enlo said quickly. He didn't have long before Revi returned. He would not waste the time by sending her back to her rooms. A plan formed in his thoughts. "No, let's go for a walk, work out some of your restless energy." He said this with a smile fixed into place, one that had melted many Elyri women's hearts. Kienna blushed and looked down.

She was not unaffected by his charms; he just had to figure out how to get past her walls.

"Come." He took her hand and drew her up.

She didn't protest, though she tugged her hand away quickly. He allowed it; this was not the time to push a boundary.

"I want to show you something," he said. "Are you up for an adventure?"

That made her brows draw together with a delightfully curious expression, and he suppressed a grin. He would lure her outside with her curiosity, then perhaps he could win her over a bit more with some well-timed heroics.

"An adventure?" she repeated as they left the library. She glanced over the hallway leading them to the rear door of the castle. "And how are we going to have an adventure in the gardens, exactly?"

He slid a sideways smirk at her. "Who said we were going to the gardens?"

Her mouth puckered as she puzzled over that enigmatic statement, but she didn't say anything else. Not right away, at least. When they reached the wall, though, she halted.

"I am not supposed to leave the castle grounds." Her eyes flicked around like an angry Revi would appear at any moment.

"You are not supposed to leave the Winter Court," Enlo countered. "The beast won't know if you go a little way beyond the castle walls."

Kienna's expression said she clearly did not believe that.

"We'll be back soon." He gave his voice the perfect balance of coaxing and daring. "We aren't going very far beyond the wall."

She hesitated but stepped forward reluctantly, casting one more glance back at the castle. "All right. So long as we don't go too far."

Enlo held the small gate open for her and shut it behind the both of them with a quiet clink. The evergreens towered beyond the wall, quiet sentinels that only served to remind Enlo of all the Winter Court had lost. Many were green, but the browning boughs interspersed were too many, a quiet plea of despair showcasing the desperation that hummed in the air alongside the curse's magic.

Enlo guided Kienna forward under the trees' shade, which was at least a cool reprieve from the summer sun. They walked in silence, the air still and hushed. Even the birds seemed to be sleeping in this hot hour.

As promised, they didn't have to go far before they reached their destination. It was nothing spectacular, just a simple gazebo that had been built beyond the castle walls. It seemed a bit useless to build something for shade in the middle of the forest, but still, it looked quaint.

And, more to Enlo's purposes, it was old, and therefore *accidental* heroics would not go amiss here.

Kienna drank in the sight as they drew closer, her eyes wide, and her mouth slightly ajar in childish wonder. Enlo resisted the urge to roll his eyes. Humans were far too easy to impress.

"This is beautiful," she breathed.

That seemed to stretch it as far as Enlo was concerned, but he merely smiled and gestured her closer under the arch of the gazebo until they stood in the very center. The roof was solid. Intricate carvings adorned the posts and the eaves.

Something prickled against the back of his neck. He froze and looked over his shoulder, but he could see nothing under the shade of the trees. The forest was still. Perhaps too still.

He shrugged the feeling off and turned back to Kienna. She was staring up at the gazebo's ceiling in delight.

Enlo looked up as well, though his study was less of admiration and more searching for the ideal spot for his charade—where the wood was oldest, the most worn.

There. One of the beams leading from the center of the gazebo to the outer rim was partially eaten away by insects. That would do for his purposes nicely. He didn't have nearly as much magic as Revi did, so he couldn't afford to waste it on sturdy wood.

Kienna wandered as she examined the carvings adorning the gazebo. The scenes were familiar to Enlo: creatures cavorting amidst snowy trees, all interspersed with frostroses that still gleamed silvery despite the wooden depiction. Frostroses couldn't help being glorious in every iteration.

Enlo moved to the side and leaned against a post as he watched Kienna circle the gazebo.

He casually made his way to the post nearest his chosen beam. His reflexes were fast, but he didn't actually want her to get hurt. He didn't know how quickly his magic would bring the wood down.

She was nearly in position. As soon as he had done his little act, they could make their way back to the castle—hopefully with more warmth and openness from her toward his advances, in gratitude for saving her life. Peril did wonders for bonding people.

Kienna glanced over her shoulder. Her mouth was opening to speak when her eyes widened, focusing on something beyond Enlo. Terror washed over her face.

A cold feeling already freezing his insides, Enlo turned to look in the shadows of the trees. Barely discernible, except for its glowing red eyes, stood a *zruyed*.

Enlo swore in Elyri. His hand went to his waist, but of course he hadn't worn his sword. He wasn't like Revi of the past, who'd felt the need to carry a weapon everywhere, and this was only supposed to be a short excursion out to win Kienna over a little more.

Snuffling to the left. Enlo whipped around. Another monster approached, jaws dripping with acidic slobber.

Instinct and fear kicked him into motion. He threw his arm out to the side. "*Lezspyr.*"

A spear of ice materialized in his hand. He drew his arm back and hurled the spear at the first creature. His aim was true. The spear buried itself in the beast's shoulder before disintegrating to a mist that was sucked into the creature's skin.

Enlo swore again. How could he have forgotten their immunity to magic? Not immunity—that wasn't the right word. They were fueled by it, as evidenced by the brighter glow to the beast's eyes and the way it bared its teeth in what almost resembled a grin.

Enlo had no weapon, and he would only be helping the enemies by using his magic. The two beasts prowled closer. In three steps, Enlo was at Kienna's side. She hadn't moved a muscle, her eyes still wide and pinned on the first *zruyed*. She was the prey, frozen in place.

"We have to run," Enlo said. "We don't have anything to fight them with." She didn't look at him as he spoke, and he grabbed her arm. "Kienna, do you hear me? We need to get back to the castle. They can't get past the walls."

"I wasn't supposed to leave the castle grounds," she whispered.

Enlo stifled the growl that wanted to rise up. Leave it to a human to freeze in the face of danger.

He checked the position of the *zruyeds* again. They prowled closer with every step, with the slow assurance that their prey had nowhere to run.

In a quick motion, he swept Kienna up and around onto his back, eliciting a quiet yelp from her. He burst into movement in the direction he and Kienna had come from. They had to get back to the castle. It wasn't far. If they could just get back to the wall—

Enlo lurched back as a third monster lunged in front of him, blocking his path. His grip on Kienna tightened as he retreated back to the gazebo. Back toward the other monsters.

He never should have brought her out here. His scheme would have been effective but was not worth truly risking her life. She was the key to the Winter Court's freedom.

Why were there *zruyeds* so close to the castle?

A tingle of awareness swept over him, chilled as a morning frost. A *zruyed*'s snarl cut off sharply, drawing the gaze of the *zruyed* in front of Enlo.

He took the opportunity to return to the gazebo's center, shrugging Kienna to her feet and turning to see the new threat. But even before he set eyes on him, Enlo knew.

He knew by the chill along his neck and the dying snarls of the *zruyeds* as they launched themselves at the greater threat.

Revi was here.

CHAPTER 22

REVI

R evi ripped through the *zruyeds*, hardly even aware of what he was doing. Fury governed his movements; he was more wolf than man at that moment. Kienna's floral scent spurred him forward. It was a smell that he never should have encountered mixed with the acrid tang of the monsters, and the combination drove his vision red. He took down the first in a single sweep and lunged at the second. He could smell a third across the clearing, beyond Kienna. A threat. His current foe bit down into his shoulder, and he snarled, bucking it off and tearing through its throat. The body dropped as he turned toward the third one.

This monster, it seemed, had the heart of a coward, for Revi could smell the terror on it before it turned tail and vanished into the forest. Unacceptable. These monsters had come to the heart of his Court, to his very castle, and they had threatened Kienna.

He took off after it, closing the distance, gaining, leaping onto its back and burying his teeth in its flesh. It didn't even get to put up a fight before he had finished it.

He lifted his snout to the air and breathed deeply. The threat was eliminated. He left the body where it had fallen, turning and stalking back to the clearing. Red still clouded the edges of his vision; adrenaline still pulsed through him. The need to fight, to make something bleed, was a steady thrum at the back of his mind.

There they were. Kienna, frozen in place, hair falling loose from her braid and ruffling around her shoulders, scent tinged with fear. He didn't want to consider the source of that fear.

Beside her, against Revi's express wishes, stood Enlo. Somehow his cousin had found a way around his promise.

"You," he growled. He wasn't even sure whom he was speaking to. Rage pulsed through him toward both of them.

Enlo stepped forward, placating hands raised in a gesture that only made Revi angrier.

"We didn't know there would be *zruyeds* so close to the castle, cousin," he said in Elyri. "I never would have brought her out here if—"

Revi snarled, cutting Enlo off and making Kienna flinch.

"You promised," he said, also in Elyri. "You promised to stay away from her."

"I never sought her out," Enlo countered, his shoulders tensing.

Revi scoffed. He started pacing in front of them. "Since when do you use your silver tongue on *me*, cousin? You promised, and I trusted you."

Enlo crossed his arms mulishly. "We finally have someone new at the castle for the first time in years, since this curse began, and you expect me to completely avoid them? *She* found *me*, Revi. She sought me out."

A snarl ripped from Revi as those words stabbed into him. She hadn't even known Enlo existed, but of course she had sought him out. He would always be more charming, more appealing to everyone than Revi was.

Revi turned to Kienna and switched to her language. "Why did you leave the castle grounds?"

Her fear had ebbed, and she stood, brow furrowed, looking between Revi and Enlo as if trying to puzzle something out. At Revi's words, her gaze snapped to him.

"He said it wouldn't take long and we wouldn't be going far," she said. "But I should have kept my promise. I'm sorry."

The sincerity in her tone drained the fight from Revi's body. He couldn't stay angry at her, but he didn't want to see her, either, standing too close beside Enlo. They looked perfectly matched. Beautiful and unmarred.

"You bring only torment into my life," he muttered in Elyri. The comment earned a sharp look from Enlo. Of course it would. Revi could do nothing right regarding Kienna in Enlo's eyes.

"What were those things?" Her gaze skittered toward, but didn't quite reach, the corpses beyond the gazebo.

"Something that should never have gotten so far into my Court." A shadow of a growl had returned to his voice, but there was no heat to put behind it anymore. With the adrenaline fading, his body ached. He hadn't slept in days, not since before he'd been wounded during his last skirmish, and he'd only stopped to hunt and shift into a wolf form on his return journey. Without the bloodlust pushing him, making it back to the castle would be a trial in itself.

"Come." He took a step and swayed, the world spinning around him.

"Beast?" Kienna's voice rang out in alarm. "Are you all right?"

"Come back to the castle," Revi said, leaving her question unanswered. He wasn't, but she didn't need to know that.

"Revi." Concern lined Enlo's tone. "What's wrong?"

Revi only growled, forcing the last of his strength to keep him upright as he stalked from the gazebo toward the castle. He hadn't even made it to the trees where the third *zruyed* lay when his legs gave out. The last thing he remembered was the scent of fear on the air again and Kienna's frantic voice.

CHAPTER 23
KIENNA

Kienna didn't sleep well after the monster attack, and her dreams... well, they were either nightmares replaying the horrible events, or, when she did dream of her cottage, it was all hazy. Her prince never came. She'd make tea, but then she'd sit alone until it went cold.

A few times, she thought she saw something out the window—but when she moved to check to see if it was him, there was no one there. And the feeling that came over her when this happened was... unnerving, like someone had stepped too close into her personal space. It was a feeling she'd never experienced with her prince—not in her dream, at least.

But he never came. She hadn't seen him in the waking world, either. She'd avoided him, truth be told. After how angry the beast had been upon seeing them together at the gazebo, she feared that he'd react poorly if he found out she'd spent any more time with her prince. The beast was confined to bed, but Zoya and the other servants were, ultimately, loyal to him, not to Kienna or her prince.

Besides, the growing certainty that the man she'd found in the waking world *wasn't* her prince wouldn't leave her. She couldn't understand most of their conversation at the gazebo, but he hadn't spoken to the beast as a captive would. He'd even called the beast by his name, if Kienna wasn't mistaken. She'd wondered for weeks what the rest of the beast's name was. Rev-something.

Revi, the prince—the man—had said. She liked how that name sounded. Strong. It fit the Winter Prince.

But if the man she'd found wasn't her dream prince, who was? Her mind returned to the question constantly, taunting her with glowing blue eyes and a deep, rich voice.

Could it be... Revi? The Winter Prince, walking her dreams in his true form instead of as a beast?

The idea fit, somehow. He had never acted as beastly as he seemed to think he did. Once she'd grown accustomed to speaking to a massive creature that looked like it could eat her... she'd begun to realize how deeply he cared for his Court. How he treated *her* with respect, even kindness. Yes, he was somewhat bristly and proud, but he was good beneath all of that.

Just like her dream prince.

But if the Winter Prince was her dream prince, why hadn't he told her?

And where did the other man fit into it all—and why had he let her believe he was someone he wasn't? He was a prisoner, he'd said that much—

That had been what he'd said, hadn't it? During their very first conversation in the waking world, when she'd found him in his study. She couldn't remember the exact words he'd said. Maybe he hadn't. Wording was so important with these blasted fae.

The whole mystery had something to do with the summer drought hanging over the Court. She was certain it did. She was missing vital information, and it wholly frustrated her.

She had no idea how to go about attaining the information she wanted, though. Short of outright asking, but Revi never answered her questions so easily as that. And the other man would almost certainly mislead her, even if he couldn't lie outright.

No. She would have to suss it out herself. Maybe if Revi visited her dreams, she could sneakily gather information there. Or maybe she could go visit him during the day, if the healers would let her by. She'd had no luck with that as of yet.

Until he healed, her dreams would have to suffice.

If he ever returned to them.

Tonight, though, when she woke in her cottage, she found herself reaching for *two* cups again, and the habitual motion sent a spear of excitement through her. Her mind seemed to know when she would need a second cup before she did.

Sure enough, a knock came at the door only a few minutes later. Kienna threw it open and let herself drink in the sight of her prince. He was so familiar, with his long silver hair and glowing blue eyes, and yet...

"Are you all right?" She threw open the door. "Here, come sit."

He stepped inside, hand clenching the doorframe for a moment before he moved to take his usual chair at the table. He didn't say a word, his silence worrying her nearly as much as his leaning on his surroundings. He wasn't chatty, necessarily, but he'd always greeted her before, or at least asked if he could enter. Never this stretching quiet.

She studied him as she gathered the tea. He was still inhumanly beautiful, still broad-shouldered, but it did seem like he was less *there* than usual. If he truly was Revi, then it made sense he'd be weak, still healing, in dreams as well as the waking world.

"You haven't answered my question," she said quietly, pushing a teacup across the table to him.

He lifted it to his lips and took a sip, eyes shutting as he swallowed. "Thank you."

She curled her hands around her cup. What could she ask to earn the answers she ached for? He'd seen her with the other man. Maybe... "Did... did the beast have you punished? Are you injured?"

He blinked at her slowly, as if his mind was having trouble processing the question. Maybe he hadn't assumed she thought the other man was her dream prince.

"I know he couldn't have done anything to you himself," she continued, "with how he's..." She bit her lip. Here she was, most likely talking to the beast—to Revi—about his own injuries that were entirely her fault. He'd only fought those monsters to protect her. The thought pushed a wall of guilt up in her.

"And 'how' is he?" he asked, expression unreadable.

It wasn't hard to produce a frown for him. She needed him to give her more clues. She needed to know if he was Revi, the beast. The Winter Prince. "He's still unconscious. How do you not know this? Have they locked you away?"

He shook his head, something flickering in his gaze.

"No one will tell me anything." Kienna rubbed her finger along the rim of her teacup. "Only that he's injured and needs rest, then they send me on my way."

His brows shot up. "You've tried to see the beast?"

"Yes," she admitted. Would it upset him to hear she'd tried to visit him? He'd been angry with her, but understandably so, given that not keeping her promise had led to such catastrophic results. She wrapped her arms around her middle. Saying these things *to* him—if he was indeed Revi—left her feeling incredibly vulnerable. "He saved my life. Our lives. I thought... I couldn't bear the thought that he was dying because of that."

"I—" Her prince cut himself off and turned sideways in his chair, almost as if he wanted to get up and start pacing. "His injury isn't your fault," he said after a moment, not meeting her eyes. "He sustained it days ago, and the venom had time to work through his body before he returned to the healers."

"Oh." Relief warred with a new flood of worry with that news. It almost made her feel worse to know it was an old injury. No wonder he was still on bedrest.

But that sounded like knowledge only Revi or his healers would know. Could she trust it as a confirmation?

She peered at him, not wanting to miss even the most minute change to his expression. "I thought you didn't know he was injured. Why would they tell you those details when they wouldn't tell me?"

His jaw clenched, and his fingers tightened on the teacup, turning white.

When it became clear he had no intention of answering, Kienna blew out an irritated breath. "I wish... I wish there weren't so many secrets here."

"What secrets do you think there are?" he asked, an odd catch to his voice.

She jerked to standing. "Between the mysterious drought, the beast's past, *you*, and my presence here, it all feels connected. Why? Why does he keep prisoners? He's not cruel to—"

He cut off her tirade. "The beast doesn't keep prisoners." He looked almost hurt at her words.

She turned and stared at him for a moment. "What am I if not a prisoner? I'm treated well, but I'm trapped here. I wouldn't even mind if it weren't for you. You said yourself that you're a prisoner. And the first time I found—" She stopped and choked. The words about finding the other man the first time wouldn't come, no matter how she wanted them to. She switched tactics. Let him continue to believe she thought the other man was her dream prince. "Why did you say you were one before, but not now?"

"I have never told you I was a prisoner," he said slowly, rising to his feet.

She threw up her hands in frustration; it was easy to do, considering her frustration was very real, even if she was leading him along on ideas she didn't really hold. "That doesn't make any sense! Perhaps you didn't use those exact words, but you *did*."

"I did?" His voice was incredulous, but then he froze, his entire countenance turning to stone. "Did *I*?" This time it came out as almost a whisper, the emphasis on the *I*. He didn't even seem to be talking to her anymore.

She watched an entire play of emotions cross his face. Anger, disbelief, hurt. She bit her lip. Whatever realization her prince had just had, she could only guess at. Had he realized something about the other man's role in all of this?

If only he'd share it with her, because she had no clue.

His movements abrupt, he turned toward the door.

"I must go." He made it there in three strides, showing more energy than he had since arriving. He stopped with his hand on the door handle and turned back to her, his eyes seeking hers.

"Don't trust your eyes," he said. "Please. Please, trust *me*."

A hysterical-edged laugh burst from her. This new world she found herself in was truly going to drive her mad. She'd gotten more reaction from him than ever before, but still he told her nothing. "You won't even tell me your name. How could I trust someone who won't trust me in return?"

Pain flashed in his eyes, and then he was gone. Kienna stood staring at the door long after he left, until she woke from her dream.

CHAPTER 24
ENLO

Enlo waited outside of the door to Revi's quarters. He couldn't ignore a summons from his cousin and prince, but he didn't want to have whatever conversation they were about to have in front of the healers, so he waited.

He waited for them to fuss over Revi, to give him a mixture of their meager healing magic, tinctures, and herbs to fight back the poison, and only when those healers ducked past him from the room did Enlo step forward through the doorway.

Revi, in wolf form, lay on his side on the massive bed in the center of the room, bandages wrapped over his silver fur. He was still, so still that Enlo thought he was sleeping at first, until, without opening his eyes, he spoke.

"I was beginning to think you would lurk in the hall all day."

Enlo gave a careless shrug, despite the fact Revi couldn't see it. "Honestly, everything they're using on you smells atrocious. I don't know how your nose can handle it."

Revi grunted.

Enlo entered the room a little farther, stopping well short of the bed.

Revi had been unconscious much of the past few days, and they hadn't spoken since the forest. Enlo could guess what this meeting was about.

Except Revi seemed too calm. Revi didn't do calm well, and Enlo found it more disconcerting than blustering anger would have been.

"How long?" Revi said. Enlo looked up to see one glowing blue eye fixed on him. "How long, Enlo, have you been going behind my back?"

Enlo stiffened at the implied accusation in those words. "I want the curse broken."

"And so you sabotage it? You were the one who insisted I make this arrangement with the human man. You were the one pushing me to woo *her*." Revi lifted his head from the bed, looking at Enlo straight on. He radiated with fury, but it was a still fury, quiet and freezing instead of Revi's usual blizzard.

"I only want to help," Enlo hedged.

"How was hindering me helping?"

"At least I was doing something," Enlo snapped. "At least I wasn't just sitting around scaring her, pushing her away. Your pride is going to get us all killed. The Winter Court can't wait for you to abandon it when we're all dying. You need to care about someone more than yourself!"

"I have *always* cared." Revi rose to his feet for a second before collapsing back on the bed.

"Not enough." Enlo threw out a hand. "You've never cared enough to actually try to break the curse in the only way possible without me pushing you. You are so tied up in the idea of fixing it all alone, content to let our Court suffer."

Revi snarled. "I have never been content—"

"You did nothing useful for years!"

"I tried dozens of ways to break the curse, or have you forgotten?"

Enlo scoffed. "You never once tried to go find a human to fall in love with you to break the curse."

"Because no one could love me!" Revi roared, and the force of his words pushed Enlo back a step. "*No one* is going to love a monster. If that is the only way to break the curse, then it has been impossible to break since the very beginning."

The pain in Revi's voice echoed against something in Enlo's own heart, but he hardened himself against it. Pain was no excuse for Revi's choices.

He pitched his voice lower. "Then why are you so angry about me seeing Kienna?"

Revi's sides were heaving. He didn't look at Enlo.

The silence stretched.

"If there's nothing else, Your Highness."

Revi only turned his head farther away. Enlo gave the smallest of bows and strode from the room. Anger vibrated in his every pore. He couldn't take it anymore. His cousin might be too blinded by his own hubris to save the Court, but Enlo wasn't, and he would sacrifice anything—any*one*—to see it done. No cost was too high.

CHAPTER 25
KIENNA

Kienna woke in her cottage, but something felt wrong. Wrong was too strong of a word, her mind told her. Nothing was wrong. But something was undeniably different. The pressing sense pushed in on her again.

She set about making tea, and her pulse quickening at the thought of seeing Revi again. She'd been turned away by his healers each time she'd tried to visit him during the day. And with how he'd left the night before, she didn't know what to expect from him today.

Instead of a knock at the door, a voice called out, making Kienna jump.

"Kienna, won't you let me in?"

She moved to the door and swung it open. Her smile froze in place at the sight of the man standing there.

Icy blue eyes, tall and lean, short hair that flopped across his forehead in a disheveled, charming way. He was familiar, but he looked wrong. This was not Revi. This was the other man, the one from the waking world.

She couldn't believe she'd ever mistaken them before. Her memories of her dream prince were always hazy during the day, but seeing him here, now, when she remembered her dreams perfectly, the differences were clear. They looked so alike they could have been brothers, or at the very least cousins. But this man was too lean, his hair too short. His eyes lacked the strange glow to their blue hue.

He didn't wait for her to greet him. He moved forward, pushing her back a step, his smile warm and his gaze intense. "I'm sorry I haven't come recently. Things have happened."

"Come in." She took another step back, allowing him entrance so she could shut the door, and cleared her throat. She wasn't sure how he'd ended up here instead of Revi, but she would do her best to take advantage of the opportunity. "Things? Have you learned something to do with the beast's injury? Or with those monsters we saw outside the wall? Is it something to do with the drought? Please tell me; I want to help."

He nodded. "My magic is... connected to the beast's. He rules this Court currently, but for me to take my rightful place, the curse must be broken."

Kienna's heart thrummed in her chest. At last someone was giving her answers. But... were they true answers, or was he twisting his words like he had before?

Her mind raced to parse through his words, trying to pull the facts from the rest.

A curse would certainly explain things—namely the drought.

"How do you break the curse?" she asked, her voice breathless. She hoped he assumed it was from excitement, not the tension that coursed through her.

He shook his head. "*You* break the curse."

Kienna blinked. That certainly wasn't the answer she had been expecting, but it would explain her presence in the Winter Court. But... it didn't fit his previous words. Alarm bells rang in her mind. Something didn't fit. "If I can break the curse, then why would the beast bring me here?"

"If you break the curse for *him*, he will continue to rule the Winter Court. But if you break the curse for *me*..." The man stepped forward, bringing his hands up; one wrapped around her waist, the other moved to cup her cheek. She tried not to startle at the sudden contact. "I need your help, Kienna. I need your help gaining my rightful place."

This man, who looked so like Revi they could have been brothers... wanted to steal Revi's throne? Was what he implied true? Did the throne rightfully belong to him, or had he just deluded himself into believing that to justify moving against Revi?

She didn't want to believe Revi had stolen the throne. He... couldn't have, could he?

But if he hadn't, this man was trying to pull her into a betrayal of the worst kind.

She was going to be ill.

"What will happen to the beast?" she managed to ask.

Something flashed across Enlo's face. "Don't fret over his fate. It's inconsequential compared to all the innocents of the Court."

She held back her questions. She was most definitely fretting over his fate. Someone had to, if his own family would betray him.

"I don't understand how *I* can help you win back your throne," she said, biting her lip.

"Just trust me." He brushed a thumb across her jaw. The motion sent shivers through her.

Trust him, he said. Just like Revi had asked her time and again.

The question came unbidden. "What's your name?"

He gave her a bemused smile. "Enlo."

Something twisted in her. How easily he gave it to her. Why hadn't Revi been so quick to trust her with his name?

"How do I break the curse, Enlo?"

Delight gleamed in Enlo's eyes. "You break the curse by marrying me."

Kienna swallowed. The cottage suddenly felt too hot. "I... What?"

"The curse can only be broken by love," Enlo said. "You declare your love for me and vow to give your life to me, and the curse will break."

It seemed so simple. Was that why Revi had never told her anything? Did he believe she couldn't love him?

"What if my feelings are not strong enough?" She turned from Enlo, breaking eye contact and moving away from his hands. She needed space from him.

She needed Revi.

"Love is a choice, Kienna. If you choose to love me to the point of self-sacrifice, the magic will recognize that."

"But then..." She twisted her hands together. She didn't have to feign her anxiety. "Then I would have to stay here forever."

"Yes," Enlo said. "But wouldn't staying here be better than going back to loss?" The words were casually spoken, but they slammed into Kienna's chest with the force of a hammer.

She whirled to look at him. "What do you mean?"

His eyes widened. "I'm sorry. I didn't mean to…" He shook his head. "No, it's better that you know. It's better that I show you. When your father plucked that rose and made that bargain, he tied himself to this Court…"

He trailed off, grimacing, and stepped toward the window. He passed a hand over the glass, and it frosted instantly; a hazy image began to appear. Kienna followed as if pulled on a string. She was absolutely certain she didn't want to see what he was about to show her, but she couldn't draw away. She had to know.

The frost crystalized and changed into a new image—her father, frail and weak in his bed at home. His skin was sallow, his cheeks gaunt.

Kienna stared at the image as her world crumbled around her.

"If you won't do it for me, Kienna," Enlo murmured, "if you won't do it for all the innocents in my Court, do it for your father. There's not much time left."

If this was true… the Court's internal strife felt distant in comparison. She couldn't let her father die.

And yet… this man had to be deceiving her. She couldn't bear to think any of his words about Revi were true. Revi had proven himself to her, time and again. She hadn't earned his trust enough to hear the truth from him, but his actions had earned *her* trust. He at least deserved her faith in him until she could verify all of this with him. If he would tell her anything.

She closed her eyes. Pain consumed her heart. She just needed to know who was true here. Was it Revi, with his proud yet kind manner? Or was it Enlo, who begged for her help with his honeyed words?

She'd find a way, *somehow*. She'd get truth from Revi. He wouldn't tell her about the Court's curse if history was anything to go by, but if she asked him about her father, surely he'd give something away. She just needed something to verify Enlo's story—or prove it false.

How she hoped it was false on all counts.

She opened her eyes to Enlo's keen gaze pinned on her. She stepped back and rubbed her arms. "Make the preparations. I'll find you tomorrow."

If he noticed that she hadn't actually sworn her hand to him, he didn't press the issue. Instead, he beamed at her, taking her hands in his. She forced herself not to rip them away.

"Together we will save the Winter Court, Kienna."

She shared a smile with him, even as her heart twisted in her chest.

CHAPTER 26

REVI

Revi was sick of his healers. They'd let Enlo visit, and his steward, but only for brief spurts—the bare essentials to keep the Court functioning, they said.

Revi didn't want to see Enlo, and his steward was too busy following his orders to exchange pleasantries.

Pleasantries weren't what he wanted, anyway.

He wanted to see Kienna. He craved her smile, her gentle touch. He'd barely managed to visit her a few nights before; dreamwalking took more finesse than he had in him in his current state, and that dream had left him too drained to repeat since.

So it was to his complete delight when her voice clashed—quietly—with his healers outside his door shortly after he woke.

He pushed himself to his feet, easing himself off his bed with a pained huff. He made his way to the door and nudged it open.

The two healers and Kienna turned to him, their argument lost at the sight of him on his feet.

"She may enter," he growled in Elyri.

"Your Highness, you really need—"

"A visitor to entertain me so I don't die from boredom." He turned a glare on the healers. "Go find yourself breakfast. Lady Kienna and I will be fine for an hour."

They paled at his wolfish ire and bowed deeply, fleeing without another word.

He resisted the urge to sag against the wall. If one glanced back and saw, they'd overrule him, prince or not.

Instead, he turned, leaving the door open for Kienna. "Come sit," he said in Kasmian Common, unsure how much of the Elyri exchange she'd understood.

He returned to his bed on unsteady legs, climbing up and dropping heavily. He was stronger than he'd been, but definitely nowhere near his full strength.

"You're awake." Kienna forewent the chair by the bed, instead settling beside him. Her hands moved toward him, but she stopped herself short of touching him. He wished she hadn't. "No one would let me see you while you were healing. I was so worried."

Her words twisted something in him. The idea of this beautiful, kind woman worrying about him was almost more than he could bear.

"I apologize," he said after a moment, "for the way I lost my temper in the forest. I was not myself."

She shook her head wildly, making her hair sway around her face. "*I'm* sorry. I should have kept my word."

He grunted. She should have, but he had already made his thoughts on that clear, so he said nothing else. And he'd never explained the dangers of venturing beyond the walls to her. He had only himself to blame for that, like so many other things.

"How are you feeling?" Her hands inched toward him again, finally daring to rest on his fur; it made him want to lean into her and rumble in pleasure.

"I'm healing."

"Good. That's... that's good." She smiled, but there was something about her expression that seemed anything but good.

He studied her. "What's wrong?"

She bit her lip.

Something protective—murderous, perhaps—rose in him. "Did Enlo hurt you?"

Her brows drew together briefly before she shook her head. "No one's hurt me. I'm just... worried about the Court. About the drought. Won't you tell me what causes it?"

He gave a tired laugh. "Questions again?"

"Yes." She sounded frustrated. "Let me help you. I can't if I don't know the truth."

The truth. He wasn't sure what the truth was. Maybe that she'd somehow gone from a nuisance to him to a comfort, a presence he ached for. She represented hope—and not only so his Court would revive, but that he could be what she believed he could. But he barely knew how to make sense of that thought, much less felt at ease to share it with her.

No. He wouldn't make everything worse by baring those nebulous sentiments to her.

"Do not worry yourself with Elyri matters," he muttered, looking away.

Her sigh was heavy in the air. Laden with disappointment. But he couldn't pull himself apart to examine his own feelings while she watched, especially not when he didn't know how he would look when he understood enough to piece himself back together.

"I... I dreamed of my father last night." He glanced back at her. She shifted, her gaze dropping to her hands. "That he's horridly ill. I know it was only a dream, but a part of me is afraid. What if it isn't? What if he dies and I never get to say goodbye?"

Just like that, every other thought halted.

"You want to go home to him." The words came out flat, stiff.

Hope lit her eyes, but she shook her head.

"I know I can't. I made a bargain to stay here for a year and a day, and I'll see that through." For her father. The words hovered unspoken in the air. Even now, after all this time, she wasn't here for Revi. She was here for her father, to save him from a worse fate. "But perhaps if you'd just let me use the kindred stone I brought with me—"

"You can." Suddenly he was so very tired. Tired of the charade of pretending there was any hope of winning Kienna's heart. She could never love a beast, but—

The truth sliced into him, all sense of uncertainty stripped away in light of the certainty of losing her.

The truth was that he cared about her. She was joy and hope and light in his life. He was—he hardly dared admit it, even to himself—in love with her. Hopelessly, since she would never return his feelings. And that impossibility was achingly obvious, mocking him at every turn.

He cared about her. And he didn't want her to suffer with the rest of his Court as his magic faded and summer consumed them, as it was and would inevitably continue doing, without her returning his love. Better to send her home. There was no point in dragging her down with his doomed Court.

"You can," he said again into the stillness of the room. "With my magic, you could go home. You could be there today."

She had frozen at his words. "I could go home?" she whispered.

"With my true name, you would have access to my magic. Magic you could use to travel there instantly." He didn't add that doing so would take most of his magic out of him, and with how the magic was fading from his Court, he wasn't entirely sure he could replenish it. Or how the Court would fare with a vacuum of magic, however brief.

But if she left, all hope left with her anyway. Maybe it would be better to let his Court die quickly—as it probably would if his magic was completely drained away—instead of this slow, painful burning one day at a time.

"Thank you," she said fervently. "I'll come back. I promise."

He nodded. There would be nothing to come back to, but he didn't have the heart to tell her that. He didn't want her to stay out of a sense of obligation.

"What do I do? When can I leave?"

He looked away. As beautiful as her hope was, he couldn't bear to watch it bloom across her face.

"You can leave now, if you want," he admitted, his voice low.

There was only a moment's hesitation before— "I do." She was unable—if she even tried—to conceal the eagerness in her voice. "Yes, please. What do I do?"

He swallowed down the protests that wanted to rise in his throat. He didn't want her to go. He was not ready. He would never be ready.

"First you say my name, my true name," he said instead, working to keep his voice neutral.

Her gaze flew up to his. "Your true name?"

"Every Elyri has a name they give most people, and a true name they never share—because it gives the speaker power over them."

Her eyes widened. They were as deeply green as ever, with her golden hair like the sun around her face.

"My true name is..." He closed his eyes. "Reviam."

"Reviam." The name was almost reverent on her lips. It had never sounded sweeter.

He cleared his throat. "And then this phrase: '*a pocheska suknish.*'"

"*Reviam 'a pocheska suknish.*" She spoke the Elyri words gingerly, and a shudder went through him as his magic responded, reaching for her of its own accord.

She had complete power over him now, and she probably didn't even realize it.

"Good," he said. "Now, your father's name, and *vozidnytsa*. Practice that before you add his name to it."

She repeated the phrase until Revi was satisfied with her pronunciation and gave her a nod. "Now add his name and focus on him in your mind. Once you say it, it may take a few moments. Magic for me is instantaneous, but when you're using it, there might be a delay."

She hesitated. "Will it hurt?"

"It will be cold," he said. "My magic is always cold, but it should not hurt you."

She nodded, pressing her lips together and pushing her shoulders back. "I'm ready."

"Go ahead," he murmured, unable to look away from her. It was the last time he'd ever see her, and he wanted nothing more than to drink her in.

"*Colm Boden vozidnytsa.*" She blinked and looked around. "Did it..." She bit her lip. "Did it work?"

Revi could already feel the cold pull of his magic moving through him. Sluggish, slow, icy. Like it didn't want to move by someone else's will.

But it was moving. She'd be gone in moments.

"Yes," he said quietly. "Goodbye, Kienna."

"I'll be back soon," she promised. "In a few days. Just once I've made sure my father is well."

He shook his head. The magic was moving faster now, pouring from him in great drafts. "You mustn't use my magic to return. It could have devastating effects from such a distance."

Kienna opened her mouth to protest, sharp concern filling her face, but he pushed his head towards her hand, desperate for her touch one last time. The movement cut her words off.

"I'll remember you until the end. Every moment." He couldn't help a pained smile. "My favorite was the ice skating. Thank you for sharing that with me one last time."

"Revi—" But her words were lost. With a gust of cold wind that swirled around him, ruffling his fur, she was gone.

CHAPTER 27
KIENNA

Everything was cold, icy, but as he had promised, it didn't hurt her. A part of her felt like she *should* be hurting. She should be dead. It was *so* cold, like she stood in the middle of a blizzard with no protection, no shelter, no cloak, nothing, and yet somehow she was still alive.

It was over in moments. Mere moments and she went from the quiet bedroom with Revi to impossibly cold before it cleared and she was standing in the middle of a camp.

No, not a camp. An outpost. Cries rang around her as her vision tried to catch up, and then...

"Kienna?" Her father's warm, deep tone.

Kienna opened her eyes and there he was, standing before her. Not ill. Not at death's door but dressed as he always was, in his military uniform, weapon at his side.

"Kienna?" he repeated. "Is it really you?"

"I'm not some trick of fae magic, if that's what you mean," she said quietly, her mind still processing the last few moments.

The next thing she knew, she was wrapped in his arms. "Kienna," he said into her hair, crushing her to his chest. "Oh, my sweet girl, my little flower."

Tears began tracking unbidden down Kienna's cheeks. He was here. He was all right. "I thought you were ill. I thought you were at home in bed and about to die and—" Her words broke off, and she buried her head farther into his chest.

"I haven't been home since I left you at the Winter Court. I begged Queen Riona to let me man this outpost. I couldn't bear to be so far from you, knowing I had left you there, alone."

"I thought you were going to die," she repeated. It was all she could think of.

He pulled back, frowning at her, searching her face. "I wasn't the one in the clutches of the fae. Why would you think that?"

Because Enlo had told her that. Hadn't he? With an awful sort of clarity, she remembered the conversation.

No, he hadn't told her. She'd assumed. He'd *shown* her a picture of her father, much like the winter wonderland vision she'd experienced, and she had assumed the rest. He'd told her that her father's fate was tied to the Court's. But that could mean anything.

She was the one who had assumed her father was dying.

Don't trust your eyes.

She wanted to cry. Or laugh hysterically. She knew to be wary of their words, but words weren't the only way to deceive. Revi had warned her of that in her very first dream. How could she have forgotten?

Revi. Her prince. He'd confirmed it with his last comment before she vanished. She'd strongly suspected, but knowing for certain her dream prince and the Winter Prince were one and the same shifted everything in her.

She should have trusted him more fully. She should have been bolder, asked him about the curse and Enlo outright instead of hedging the topic. Instead, she had believed Enlo—a stranger, a man she had found, a man who had let her believe *he* was her prince.

Her last conversation with him, when he had come to her dream instead of Revi, played through her mind with a horrifying clarity. He wanted to take Revi's place, to break his magic, break the curse and rule the Winter Court. He couldn't break the curse without Kienna. He had said that much plainly, but that didn't mean he wouldn't try to do something against Revi.

And Revi had just given her magic to come here. He'd told her not to use the magic to return. Did he not expect her to come back at all? And the way he'd said goodbye, as if it were so very final.

What had he just done for her? What if he was too weak to fend off the other man's schemes, and it was her fault?

"Kienna?" Her father watched her with a furrowed brow. She stepped back from him and smiled, though it felt tight. Any relief she'd felt that he was whole and hale had vanished in the wake of her thoughts.

"I'm glad you're well," she said. "I truly am. I'm so relieved."

"Is your bargain broken? It must be for you to return early. Did it break because the Winter Prince did something to you?"

"No," she said quickly. "It's not. I have to return. I have to go back immediately." He opened his mouth to argue, and she placed a hand on his arm. "Please, Papa. Take me back to the Winter Court."

CHAPTER 28

ENLO

Enlo pulled himself back to his body. He dug his fingers into the arms of his chair.

Revi had sentenced the entire Winter Court to death for a *human*. It had been a ridiculous waste of his magic, and now their last hope was gone. She'd tricked Enlo, implied she'd go along with his plan—only to run to Revi first thing upon waking.

Enlo could only hope she'd come back like she'd promised Revi she would. But before then, he needed to deal with Revi. This was the final proof that Revi truly wasn't worthy to rule the Winter Court any longer. He'd be weak after using so much magic. Enlo would not waste the opportunity.

He rose from his seat and collected the axe he'd found earlier that day. The halls were empty—as they always were now. He encountered no one as he left the castle and traversed the gardens, his hand clenched around the handle of his axe. He wouldn't have long to do what he needed to do. As soon as he made the first strike, Revi would surely know. His hand tightened on the axe. He was only doing what needed to be done, though it gave him no pleasure.

Revi sending Kienna away was all the confirmation Enlo had needed. Revi was unwilling to make the sacrifices necessary for their Court.

Enlo had no such qualms.

The garden was quiet, but that was no surprise with no courtiers at the Winter Court. There was no one to wander the gardens but servants, and they rarely took advantage of that option. The fear of Revi, if something accidentally happened to his frostroses, was too strong.

The roses waited where they always were, cast in the soft morning sunlight. Enlo walked toward them slowly, trepidation filling his heart. If he did this, there would be no going back. He would kill Revi, or Revi would kill him.

The thought twisted in him like a knife to his heart. But he cut himself off from the sensation. Someone had to be willing to put the Court before their emotions.

Squaring his shoulders, Enlo lifted the axe and brought it down on the roses.

A pulse of magic shuddered through the air, much like the one from Kienna's departure, except this one held an edge of wrongness to it. Of pain. Enlo pushed away the feeling and raised the axe again.

CHAPTER 29
REVI

With Kienna's departure, Revi's legs gave out. He slumped down onto the bed, digging his claws in.

He had known the cost of the magic, but knowing and actually experiencing it were two different things. He rested his head on his paws, waiting for the weakness to pass. Waiting for a semblance of strength to return to him. It was only a few minutes before he tried to rise again. He made it off the bed, but on his first step across the floor, he collapsed, a pulse of pain shooting through him. It wasn't just the stabbing discomfort of moving while weakened. It was a lightning-hot agony that spread throughout his whole body.

A snarl escaped him. There was something deeply wrong about this pain. Dread rooted itself in his chest. What had he done? Had Kienna used more magic from such a distance despite his warning of the danger? He'd trusted her with his name, his *true* name. Perhaps she had already betrayed him. The thought tore through him, causing almost as much torment as the physical sensation. He had trusted a human with his name and... his heart. He desperately hoped this wasn't him living to regret that.

He lay on his side, chest heaving, for an indeterminate amount of time. Every time he thought to move, another wave of agony staggered through him. It felt like the very life was being ripped from him, leaving him with nothing but deep, clawing emptiness.

Enlo. He had to find Enlo. If he didn't, he was certain this rending inside him would tear him apart. He needed his cousin. He needed other magic to shore up his defenses until this passed and his strength returned. He dug his claws into the floor and forced himself to his feet. His vision clouded; he nearly blacked out when he tried to take a step forward.

He paused and waited until he was steady, and then he took another step, and another. Slowly, so slowly, making his way out toward the entrance hall of the castle. His head spun too much to try to process where he might find Enlo. But if he could just get out there, maybe he could at least find a servant who could fetch Enlo for him.

But he'd sent the healers away, and the skeleton crew of servants were probably off completing their morning duties, for he found no one. He started in the direction of the kitchens; that was his best hope, where he was most likely to find help.

He was leaning against the wall in the hallway just off the dining room when Enlo found him.

"Cousin," Revi rasped. "My magic. I need—" Talking made his head spin even worse. He paused and gulped in a breath of air. Enlo hurried forward, an axe held loosely in his hand. Revi was too weak and disoriented to wonder about that.

He tried to straighten, swaying on his feet slightly as Enlo approached.

Enlo's expression was twisted, grim. "I'm sorry, cousin."

Revi started again, barely hearing Enlo's words. He needed to explain so Enlo would know how to help him. "Something is wrong with my—"

He cut off sharply as Enlo sprang forward, swinging the axe at Revi's head.

CHAPTER 30
REVI

Adrenaline surged through Revi as the axe swung down, giving him the strength to throw himself out of its path. He staggered sideways and away from Enlo as his cousin straightened, drawing the weapon up to strike again.

"What summer-cursed madness has possessed you?" Revi snarled, backing away even as Enlo stalked forward.

"It has to be done, Revi," Enlo said grimly.

Revi searched his face, looking for any sign that Enlo was not himself, that he was possessed or controlled in some way. But his eyes were clear, his expression twisted into one of tense determination and lined with grief.

Revi stumbled back from yet another axe swing. This one cut close. So close that Revi could feel the whoosh of it against his fur. "What are you talking about?"

Enlo adjusted his grip on the axe and kept coming. It was only Revi's years of ingrained training and predator instincts that kept him out of Enlo's reach. But he was fueled with adrenaline, and that could only do so much against the agony and weakness of his shredded magic. He stumbled as often as he leaped.

"One of us has to do what it takes to save our Court." Sweat beaded on Enlo's brow, and his swings were slowing. He was only a warrior by necessity; he'd never had Revi's skills or stamina. "You have proven your loyalties are not strong enough to do what needs to be done. You sent away the Court's only hope. Our last chance is that perhaps I can do better than you."

"Do what better? Make Kienna fall in love with you?"

Enlo lunged, leaving his side wide open; Revi scampered back against every martial instinct to go in for the kill. He had no desire to hurt Enlo.

"This has nothing to do with Kienna specifically. She's just a human. She doesn't matter compared to the Court as a whole. None of us do."

Enlo's words made Revi want to snarl, but still he retreated. He couldn't fight his cousin, the closest thing he had had to a brother, his loyal—no, not loyal, apparently, but his constant companion through every year of Revi's life. The fact that Enlo did not hold the same qualms tore something foundational in Revi's body. Something broke in him. Something that could probably never be fixed.

"You wanted me to fall in love with her, and now you're angry that I did?" Revi asked.

"I wanted *her* to fall in love with *you*," Enlo said. His axe buried into a nearby doorframe. He ripped it out with a grunt. The brief hindrance gave Revi time to put more distance between them, but then Enlo resumed his purposeful stride toward Revi, coming in for another swing once he closed the gap.

Revi anticipated the movement and dodged to the side, swiping at the axe shaft and sending it spinning from Enlo's grip. He couldn't hurt Enlo, but it would be much easier to talk sense into his cousin without a sharp edge between them.

"She doesn't deserve to die with us, Enlo."

"You are the only one who has given up and decided that we are dying at all." Fire lit Enlo's gaze as he leaned in. "You may have surrendered, but I never will."

Revi's sides heaved as he struggled for breath. Adrenaline still coursed through him, but it wouldn't last forever, and beneath it, he could still feel his weakness from his previous injuries.

"When did you lose faith in me?" Revi asked, weariness seeping into his very soul. It was a deep ache, far more than physical. He wanted to groan under the weight of it. "You've always stood beside me. Always supported me."

Enlo scoffed and threw out a hand. "When I realized you would never do what our Court needed to break this curse. But I will, even if it means I have to take your place as Winter Prince. You may have doomed us, but *I* can save us. I can do what you refuse to."

Revi shook his head. "I've tried, Enlo. I tried to find another way to break the curse. I even tried to get closer to Kienna. But it was doomed from the beginning."

"*That*—that belief is why I must do this." Enlo squeezed his eyes shut and turned his head away as if to hide his pain from Revi, but it stabbed into Revi anyway. Every word cut him as deeply as it probably cut Enlo to speak them. "You gave up long ago." Enlo swept a hand out at the castle around them. "No one else saw you as the beast you see yourself as. You've always just been our Winter Prince. But you saw yourself as a beast, and you acted as such instead of doing what we needed. You took that on as your identity, wrapping it around yourself and tying your pride to the concept. And *that* is what has doomed us."

Revi studied his cousin—the way his chest heaved, the way his eyes blazed with the passion of his words, with the truth he felt in them, and Revi wanted to weep.

"You're right," he whispered. "I am a fighter, a warrior, a protector. With the curse, it became so easy to blend that identity with the forms I was trapped in. But you have always been there to remind me of the importance of being more than just a beast. Of caring for our Court in other important ways. You have always been better with people than I."

Enlo watched Revi warily, as if waiting for some trick.

Revi closed his eyes briefly and exhaled. He looked at Enlo. "And in recent times, even with this betrayal, though it shreds my heart, you have proven that your love for the Court is greater than mine." He stepped forward. Enlo leaned back as if to retreat. "If you truly believe you can fix it, then do."

He hesitated only a moment before he closed the gap between them and pressed his nose to Enlo's hand. "I give our Court to you, Enloras. I trust you. I forgive you. *Em Reviam krestolla presnyv y pocheska vannost tu Enloras.*"

This would probably be the end of him, but it felt right. Perhaps Enlo was right; perhaps he could do what Revi could not.

Enlo's eyes widened as a shock of cold zinged between him and Revi, and then, with a great shudder, a wave of heat rolled through the air, followed immediately by a blast of cold, as if Winter had come all at once.

Revi locked his knees to keep from collapsing. Unbearable agony arced through him, sharp and hot. The most he'd ever felt, at least since—

Thought shut down as it overtook his mind, tearing away every rational part of him for a moment that felt like an eternity.

And then it was over as quickly as it had come, and Revi collapsed to the floor, palms hitting the cold stone of the entryway. He stared at them, his mind too stunned to make sense of what he was seeing.

"Revi?" Enlo's voice brought him back to his senses; the shock in it mirrored his own.

Maybe he wasn't imagining things. He raised one hand, and his throat tightened. Tears sprang to his eyes. He had *hands*. He turned it over and curled his fingers, savoring how the movement felt.

"You're... you're back to normal," Enlo whispered. "You broke the curse?"

Revi gave a helpless shrug. Wherever she was, had Kienna vowed to marry him? The idea was preposterous, and he quickly discarded it. It made no sense. Behind them, a cold wind blew through the open door.

Revi and Enlo locked gazes before Revi lurched to his feet and dashed for the entrance. Enlo was faster, darting ahead of Revi, but he drew to a sharp stop on the threshold. A grin burned its way across Revi's face as he stopped at Enlo's shoulder. Thick, fat snowflakes drifted down from the sky, swirling in little eddies in the air on the cold winter wind.

"The curse is broken," Enlo whispered. "You broke the curse." His expression was unreadable. "How?"

"If I had known there was a way I could break the curse without a beautiful woman before now, you would already know." Emotion made it difficult to speak without Revi's voice cracking on the words.

Enlo opened his mouth to respond, but whatever he said, Revi missed it. A sensation that could only be described as a sharp slicing across his magical senses tore into him. He doubled over, collapsing against the doorframe. He reached out through his senses, beyond himself, into the magic in the near vicinity. Something that had been so easy before sending Kienna away, even a few moments ago before handing his throne to Enlo, pushed black spots into his vision now. But he managed it for a few brief seconds before it snapped back to him.

"*Zruyeds*," he gasped, fury giving him a new strength. "My magic is too weak to hold the border around the castle. *Zruyeds* have breached the wall."

Enlo's brows drew down sharply at the news. "How many?"

"A dozen." Revi drew in a deep breath, and then another, letting his mind fall back on his warrior training. He had no weapons; he hadn't needed them in years. A beast had no need to carry around a sword or war axe.

A beast. He nodded once, decided. The idea of returning to a beastly form turned his stomach, but he had done it before the curse, and he would do it again. He was nothing but a warrior now—not a beast, but a protector, just as he had always been. He was no longer the Winter Prince, but he would do whatever he needed to protect his Court. Just like always.

"*Zeminy*."

With a roar and the last dregs of his magic, he shifted back to a beast one last time.

CHAPTER 31
ENLO

E nlo stepped forward as Revi's familiar frostcat form appeared beside him again.

"What are you doing?" he demanded.

"The curse is broken." Revi's voice rumbled in its familiar beastly cadence. "Our people need a leader, and it's not me. I will handle this threat."

Revi didn't wait for Enlo to respond, and Enlo stared after him as he bounded across the fresh snow, leaving massive paw prints in his wake.

Enlo dug his hands into his hair. The curse was broken. The thought kept circling in his mind. *Revi* had broken the curse, Enlo suspected strongly, because of his willingness to sacrifice himself. To let Enlo lead.

He had sacrificed his days in a far more permanent way because of his love of the Court and his love of Enlo. Now he was doing it again, going to face a dozen enemies on his own. Enlo had no doubt he would die from it. He was already weak, bereft of most of his magic.

Because of Enlo.

Enlo could have everything he wanted. He could keep the throne. He could probably even spin the story to paint himself as a hero. Revi would be gone. No one would know.

But... Revi would be *gone*. His best friend. His almost-brother. The one who had always sought his opinion, had always valued him as they'd worked *together* for the Winter Court.

The clarity that came with that thought stung like a dive into a frozen river, and he suddenly understood why Revi had chosen to let Kienna leave. Saving the entire Winter Court would be meaningless if he lost Revi in the process. Enlo had never truly wanted his cousin's throne. His desperation to get out of the curse had twisted his thoughts and made him believe it was the only way to save them all.

But the curse was broken. Revi had broken it. Revi, the strong warrior, the fearless protector, the man Enlo had seen fight for his people time and again. Just like he was fighting now, while Enlo hung back. Revi had always been willing to die for his people, but Enlo had finally realized he couldn't let that happen.

He started down the steps of the castle, paused, turned around, and dashed inside, scooping up the axe forgotten on the floor before running back outside.

Revi was a maelstrom of death. He moved amongst the *zruyeds* that had converged on him in the front garden, delivering destruction the likes of which Enlo hadn't seen from him since the attacks that had led to the curse.

But at the same time, it was nothing like that, because for every two strikes Revi made, the *zruyeds* delivered one to him. Red stained his fur and the fast-growing layer of snow on the ground.

They were killing him as surely as he killed them.

Enlo leaped into the fray, striking the nearest enemy and drawing its attention away from Revi. He fought desperately, leaning into the long-buried memories of fights won against these monsters. He'd never been a great warrior like Revi, but he had held his own, and he dredged up those recollections to do so again now. He narrowly avoided one taking his head off, scrambling back and cutting into it with his axe. It dropped at his feet, and he moved in to guard Revi's back, just as he had before. One by one, the *zruyeds* fell.

Until none were left.

Enlo didn't even realize it until a pained whine cut through the silence. He whirled; Revi had collapsed, his sides heaving. His face was wan.

Enlo dropped to the ground beside Revi. In his comatose state, Revi was already shifting back to his natural form, tangled silver hair spread around him in waves.

"No, no, no!" Enlo growled. He pulled Revi onto his lap and pressed his hands to each side of Revi's head. He tapped into his newfound magic—the Court's magic, meant for the royal on the throne. It felt weak, or maybe empty, like a drought-plagued river, somehow. And it was supposed to be *Revi's*, not his.

But even as empty as it felt, it was still a large force compared to his own normal magic; his was a bowl he could draw on in small amounts. This was a torrent. Enlo almost wasn't sure how to wield it. So with all of the finesse of a blind, blundering bear, he shoved it at Revi, willing it, *begging* it to go back to its original master.

It seeped into Revi, but without proper guidance, Enlo could feel it draining out just as quickly as it entered.

He pushed more in futile hope, but when that did the same as before, he stopped. Wasting the magic wouldn't help anyone. If only Enlo hadn't destroyed Revi's roses—

His head snapped up.

The frostrose bush. He had destroyed the roses, yes, but the bush itself was still there.

He was on his feet in moments. He heaved Revi up over his shoulders, gripping one leg and one arm in front of him. He grunted as he took a step. Even as a man, Revi was massive. Enlo gritted his teeth and took another step.

Too slowly, keenly aware of the fading heartbeat against his shoulder blades, Enlo carried Revi to the eastern garden. To the frostrose bush, mangled as it was. Shame burned Enlo as he looked at it. Tears stung his eyes. He pushed the emotions away and carefully laid Revi down on the snow beside the bush. He looped one of Revi's arms up and over a stunted branch, and he curled his own fingers around Revi's to grip the plant.

He stretched out his senses toward Revi, trying to gauge if the bush was having any effect on him. The magic of the bush swirled around Revi, some even sinking into him, but his magical presence did not grow stronger. Enlo tightened his fingers over his cousin's, pressed his forehead to Revi's chest, and let silent, wracking sobs overtake him.

CHAPTER 32

KIENNA

Kienna rode hard through the forests and mountains to reach the Winter Court.

She ignored her father's urges to slow for the sake of the horses. She'd allowed brief respites, but only as long as it took for her horse's sides to stop heaving before she pushed him back into speed.

There was a horrible, aching, hollow feeling in her, and she was terrified of what it meant. The cold burned her eyes, and the whip of wind against her skin rubbed it raw, but still she did not stop.

After far too long, though it had only been a day or two of travel, they arrived.

Kienna almost didn't recognize it at first. There had been a different feeling in the air, a delicious cold zing, ever since the forest grew thick with evergreens half a day back.

But she had been waiting for evergreens dying under the heat of summer—and then suddenly they reached a wall. A familiar wall, for she had spent weeks staring at the other side of it.

Except that this wall was capped in snow, icicles hanging on any outcropping. Everything glistened in the brief winter sun that had peeked out, bright but weak compared to the summer sun she had grown accustomed to while living here.

They paused at the gates. One sat off its hinge at a crooked angle, as if broken down from the outside, and Kienna's breath left her as everything inside squeezed in alarm.

The sight set Papa and his men on high alert. She could hear the murmurs and the whisper of steel as it left the scabbards.

She turned and put a hand up. "You can't go in. It would break the bargain."

"I will not let my daughter walk knowingly into danger. Your prince may not harm you, but whatever did that"—Papa gestured with his sword toward the broken gate— "certainly will."

"Papa," she started to argue, but his gaze was steel.

"If this forfeits my life, then so be it." He raised his voice. "I go through. Know that any man who goes with me might be walking into death, and no one is dishonored if they choose to stay behind." He stared her down as he nudged his horse through the open gate.

Kienna squeezed her legs into the side of her own horse, followed by the slow *clop, clop, clop* of the rest of the men after a few moments.

She gasped as she took in the sheer beauty of the space before her. It was almost exactly like the winter wonderland her prince had shown her in her dream. Snow covered everything in a jeweled blanket. There were a few odd mounds that she didn't remember strewn across the ground, but as one of her father's men dismounted and dislodged some snow from the side of one of the mounds, she shuddered and looked away.

"I think we found the threat," she said quietly, counting them. A dozen. A dozen mounds lay scattered across the grounds.

A dozen of those monstrous beasts that her prince had saved her from once before.

Worry returned in full force. A dozen of them. Revi had taken on three to protect her and Enlo, but could he take on a *dozen*?

She had to find him. She pushed her horse forward to the bottom of the stairs leading up into the castle and jumped down, taking the steps two at a time.

Snow crunched under her feet. She couldn't help but marvel at that fact. Whatever curse had befallen the Winter Court, clearly it was gone. But at what cost? Was Revi even here anymore to greet her? Had she returned too late? She shoved open the front door; the slam of it echoed down the castle halls.

"Hello?" she cried. "Is anyone here? Zoya? Revi? Hello?" She was halfway across the room when Zoya appeared, her hair disheveled, her breath huffing.

Her eyes widened at the sight of Kienna. "My lady, you've come back."

"Where's Rev—the prince?" Kienna asked.

Zoya's face tightened in a way Kienna hated.

"The frostroses." Zoya stopped at Kienna's side. Kienna squeezed Zoya's hands in her own. "It's good to see you, my lady, but you'd best hurry. Who knows how long before—" She cut herself off, her eyes tightening further. "To the frostroses, my lady. Hurry."

Kienna squeezed Zoya's hands one more time. "My father and some of his men are outside. Please see them inside to warm by a fire and send someone to care for their horses."

Zoya gave a sharp nod, then Kienna drew her hands away, turned, and ran back outside. She ignored Papa's questions as she followed a snow-covered but familiar path from the castle doors. She heard Zoya's calm, sweet tones behind her as she approached Kienna's father, but then the sound was lost amid her own hard breathing and the crunch of snow under her boots.

She rounded the edge of the castle, then passed the bushes guarding Revi's garden from view of the castle from this angle. There. The frostrose bush looked nothing like she'd last seen it; even the glistening snow that covered it could not completely hide how mangled and destitute the bush looked.

And on the ground just beside it lay her prince.

His long silver hair, his large broad shoulders. His skin was white as snow, half covered in bandages. His eyes were closed. He looked too still. He looked... dead.

A cry broke from her. She pushed herself faster. She barely registered the man kneeling at his side.

"You returned." Enlo's voice came out ragged.

"What's wrong with him?" She dropped to her knees and cupped his face in her hands.

"A lot," Enlo said tightly. "He has very little magic. The venomous wounds inflicted by the attack a few days ago have been treated, but he grows weaker by the day. I keep pushing magic into him. But it won't last forever. He's..." Enlo swallowed, his gaze dropping to Revi's face. "He's dying."

"No," Kienna whispered. "No, Revi. You cannot die. I'm sorry I didn't see it sooner. I'm sorry I trusted this stupid man next to you instead of you. I'm sorry I left. I'm sorry I wasted your magic for no reason. But I'm here now and *you can't die*." His cheeks were cold beneath her fingers; a tear dripped down the tip of her nose and landed on his cheekbone.

"You can't die," she repeated. "Because I love you. I came back, and I want to spend my entire life with you. Whether you're a beast or whether you are my dream prince. I don't care. Just stay with me. Please."

Enlo sucked in a breath, looking between Kienna and Revi.

"Say that again," he said. "Tell him you love him. Use his name. Make your vow again."

She dragged her distracted gaze up to Enlo. "My vow?"

"You need to bind yourself to him. Maybe—" His voice broke. "Maybe it will be enough to save him."

She looked up at him, eyes wide. The cold bit at her cheeks along the lines where tears tracked down. "I'm only human. My words don't have magic. It won't do anything."

"But it *might*. If you finish the link between you two, you might be able to save him. Vow your life to him, become his wife. Use his name. Use your name, your true name."

Kienna looked back down at Revi. She'd do it in a heartbeat. But what if he didn't want this?

It didn't matter. Even if he resented her for making such a bond between them, she'd do it. He could hate her; he could send her away. He would be alive to do so, and that was all she cared about. She needed him to *live*.

She swallowed. "I'll do it, but—I don't know what to say."

Enlo didn't smile, but there was a grim hope that settled over his features. "Repeat after me. *Em*, then your name, then '*a pocheska sukerste tu Reviam.*" He spoke the phrase slowly, pausing after each word to let Kienna repeat him.

"*Em Kienna Boden 'a pocheska sukerste tu Reviam.*"

"Now kiss him."

Kienna's entire body trembled as she leaned closer to Revi. It might have been cold. It might have been nerves. It might have been shaky hope strangled by terror that this wouldn't work.

She closed the space between them and gently pressed her lips against Revi's. They were freezing but soft. She let her eyes shut as something icy zinged between her and Revi where their lips connected them, where her hands rested against his chest.

It shocked up and down her spine, through her limbs, into her heart. She gasped against him, jerking back a few inches.

He inhaled a ragged breath. His bright blue eyes fluttered open and landed on her.

CHAPTER 33
REVI

R evi was freezing. He was drifting in a glacial expanse, a chill that bit down into his marrow, but despite the lack of heat, something about the cold thrilled him and also gave a deep sense of peace that he had almost forgotten the feeling of. That cold meant he could rest. That cold meant all was right with the world.

Soft, warm lips pressed against his own. The peace he felt was joined by a sense of exhilaration. His eyes flicked open.

Leaning over him, her face filling his vision and spreading fire in his chest, was Kienna. At the sight of him, her teary face erupted into a quavering smile.

"It worked," she said. "It worked! You're alive." And then she burst into tears, burying her head in his chest. His hands came up of their own accord to stroke her hair.

He had hands. He had hands because he'd broken the curse, but hadn't he returned to a beast? To fight the...

"The *zruyeds*?" he blurted out, jerking upright and looking around wildly.

"Peace, cousin," Enlo said. He knelt a pace away, pure relief in his own expression. He raised a hand to allay Revi's panic. "They're gone."

The initial panic faded as the fight came back to Revi. Yes, he'd destroyed most of them, but he had been so weak he'd been almost overcome. He would have been if not for... He looked at Enlo.

"You saved my life."

What would have been a moment of good-natured gloating from his cousin any other time was instead filled with a grimace. Enlo averted his eyes.

"Yes, well"—he kept his tone light, but his wary, guilt-ridden expression was utterly unlike him—"it was the least I could do for trying to murder you."

A soft hiss escaped Kienna's lips. Revi found her fingers and squeezed.

"It's safe to say you're done trying to murder me," he said. "You have no need to now. The curse is broken, and the throne is yours."

"I don't want the throne." Enlo's voice was barely more than a whisper. "I don't deserve the throne."

"I meant everything I said, Enlo. I think you'll be an admirable leader."

Enlo shook his head. "No. I mean, yes." A hint of his usual smirk ghosted across his face for a flicker of a moment. "I would be a good leader." He swallowed and met Revi's gaze. "But you are already a great one. For your claims of not caring about the Court as much as I do, you made the choice that you believed would protect it the most, at the cost of your own life—just like you always have—and that action was what saved us. I don't deserve your throne, Revi, and I've never truly wanted it." He inclined his head to Revi. "So please, let me give it back."

"Are you sure, cousin?" Revi asked softly.

Enlo smiled. "I'm certain. Don't worry, I won't change my mind and try murdering you again in six months."

"That would be inconvenient," Revi agreed. He opened his mouth, then hesitated. A part of him wanted to refuse his cousin, to reject the throne.

Enlo seemed to sense this. "You fear they don't love you. But I would argue that the quiet loyalty you get from them is far stronger than anything my charm and wit has earned me."

"I have done nothing to earn it," Revi whispered.

"I think they would disagree." Enlo gestured behind Revi.

He turned. Their small staff who had stayed at the castle was hurrying up the garden path. They stopped at the sight of Revi, their eyes lighting up before giving him deep bows from where they stood.

"Be the prince they need," Enlo said. "I know you can. Besides, you won't be alone. You have a beautiful wife with an excellent sense of character. She chose you over me, after all."

Revi glanced at Kienna, who blushed deeply but met his gaze.

"Wife?" he said stupidly.

"I'm sorry," she blurted. "I'm sorry—it was the only way to save you. If you don't... you don't want me, I... I..." She stammered to a stop, her cheeks flushing even further.

He squeezed the hand he still held. "Hold that thought. I have something I must attend to first." He turned back to Enlo and gave him a nod.

Enlo didn't wait for him to change his mind again. *"Em Enloras krestolla presnyv y pocheska vannost tu Reviam."*

As the last syllable left Enlo's mouth, a surge of icy energy pulsed through Revi. He sucked in a breath. He felt ready to take on a hundred enemies, which was not how he had felt the last time he'd held this magic.

"How long was I out?" he muttered.

Enlo grimaced. "A few days."

Revi nodded. "A few days would be enough time to replenish the magic with the curse broken."

Enlo stood and gave Revi a deep bow. "To your health, Your Highness. I'll leave you two to discuss things." His tone was teasing, but there was something in his eyes that Revi didn't like.

"I'll come find you soon," he promised.

Enlo didn't respond, only inclined his head and turned toward the castle. Only when the crunch of his footsteps faded under the sound of the winter breeze around them did Revi draw in a breath and look at his bride.

His *bride*. Hope rose unbidden to suffuse his entire being.

"I don't know if Enlo told you," he said quietly, "but the curse on our Court—we thought it had to be broken by marriage."

Kienna nodded. "When he came to my dream, pretending to be dream-you, he did. But you managed it without me." She paused. "What... what was the curse, exactly?"

The words flowed over Revi's lips almost unbidden. "'Summer shall rule in Winter's land, while beast confines the heart of man, until the strongest of the weak a lifelong devotion does speak, and restores a Heart of Winter.' We thought the strongest of the weak meant a human—but apparently the leader of a group of weakened Elyri sufficed."

"And Enlo is a Heart of Winter," Kienna supplied, "because he's your... cousin?"

179

"Yes. It broke when I passed him my throne. Gave up my future to him—my life, too, because the vestiges of magic tied to the throne were all that were keeping me alive after"—Revi grimaced and glanced at the bush beside him—"he destroyed my roses and thereby my personal magic. I'm surprised I lasted as long as I did on the small ripples coming from this." He stroked a finger down the bush's nearest branch, and it gave a sad little shiver of magic in response.

"We didn't talk much before I... woke you up." She bit her lip, seeming embarrassed by her own word choice. Or, rather, probably the words she *hadn't* said. "Why did that work?"

"In an Elyri marriage, you aren't just promising to stay together, to love each other. You are linking your very souls, giving your spouse access to all your days, your magic, your life force. Linking it to mine was enough for my own life to latch onto it and pull back from the brink."

Kienna grimaced.

Revi looked away. She'd saved him, but that didn't mean she *wanted* him. She hardly even knew him. "I'm sorry. There's no way to undo it."

"I don't—" Kienna stopped, and then something crossed over her expression. It solidified. "I don't want to undo it. I didn't marry you just to save you. I *do* love you." She looked up at him from under her lashes, that sudden resolve morphing into something shy, uncertain. "I understand if you don't feel the same way, but..."

Revi chuckled, though he felt little humor. "There's that phrase again. My feelings were *never* the problem here, Kienna. I've been besotted with you since the day you arrived. The day you stared me down—a beast who could rip you to shreds—despite the fear I could smell on you." She made a face. Revi laughed. "Yes, I could smell your fear. I could hear your heartbeat, and the fact that you were so afraid and yet so brave captivated me so much that I told my charming, handsome cousin to stay away from you because I was afraid that if you met him, you'd never look twice at me. You had no *reason* to look twice at me. What woman could fall in love with a beast?" He drew his hand back and ran it through his hair to give it something else to do.

"Well, you do have rather poor manners sometimes." Her mouth twitched up in a teasing smile. "What with the way you eat, and with the fact that we're still sitting in the snow, which has definitely soaked through all of my skirt layers at this point."

Revi glanced down, chagrined, but her teasing smile caught him. She reached out gently and wrapped her fingers back around his.

"But your heart is good," she said. "You never were cruel or purposely tried to frighten me. You acted like a man, a *good* man, not a beast. Zoya sometimes told me stories of your heroics, how you saved and helped your people. And in my dreams..." At this point she blushed, her gaze flitting across his chest and back up to his eyes. "You were only ever the gentleman. I was blind for not realizing that my dream prince was *you* sooner."

"The fangs could be a bit misleading," he muttered, and she laughed. He loved the way her laugh lit up her face.

"A bit," she agreed.

"I'll still have those occasionally," he said. "I've always been able to shapeshift into any animal I wanted."

"Like a rabbit?" she asked teasingly. He made a face and cleared his throat, which only caused her to laugh again.

"It was only with the curse that I was *trapped* in animal forms, a beast to reflect my inner self, according to the Summer Queen."

"It was a good representation of your protective nature," Kienna said. "Teeth and claws, and also warm and cuddly."

He grinned and, made bolder by her words, pulled her to him, wrapping his arms around her and pressing her against his chest. She squeaked at the sudden movement before nuzzling closer, burying her head and sliding her arms around his waist.

"I take it this means you want me to stay?" she asked, a note of hesitation still lingering in her voice.

"Not only do I want you to stay," Revi said, "I want to redo those vows when I'm actually awake for them."

"What if that upsets the magic somehow?"

"Your magic is sealed. All that is left is vowing my own life to you and sealing it with another kiss. I especially look forward to that part." He used one hand to tilt her face up to look at his. "I love you. And yes, I want you to stay, to be my Winter Princess or my Winter Queen forever."

Her eyes shone. "My heart is already yours, my Winter Prince."

CHAPTER 34
ENLO

Enlo slipped down the hall, a bag of supplies slung over his shoulder and one of food pilfered from the kitchen in hand. He would have asked, if anyone had been there *to* ask. But between Kienna returning and healing Revi less than an hour ago and the ongoing snow that the Winter Elyri couldn't help but bask in after so long without—well, no one was around to ask.

And no one to stop him.

He reached the entrance hall, slowing to listen for any sign of life. The eastern exit would have been ideal—he didn't want to skirt the entire castle. But neither did he want to run into his cousin before he left. Revi would only try to talk him out of his plan. Main entrance it was.

The entryway stood empty, only faint voices floating down the hall from one of the side receiving rooms. Companions of Kienna, he guessed, by the cadence of their voices.

He crossed the hall and pulled open one of the great doors—only to come face-to-face with Kienna herself.

"Oh." She jerked her hand back from where the handle had been, eyes narrowing as she realized whom she'd met. "What are you doing?"

Enlo glanced behind her—no Revi. "Shouldn't you be with my cousin? Young love suffers from time apart."

"His steward dragged him away. I wanted to check on my father." She shifted, crossing her arms. Her attire was appropriately warm for the winter weather, but her cheeks and nose were still tinged pink from staying outside so long.

Enlo pulled the door open the rest of the way and stepped aside. "By all means. I heard their voices coming from the far-left hall."

Kienna crossed the threshold but paused as she took in his bags. "Are you... leaving?"

He glanced once more toward the open doorway. If she held him up so long that Revi came looking for her...

But he had thought about speaking with her. There were things he should say. This was clearly a sign he was meant to say them.

He sighed. "Yes."

Conflicting emotions flickered over her face—relief, suspicion, confusion. "Why?"

"I don't deserve to be here." He shifted. The words clawed up from him, unwilling to come. But if he told her, she'd tell Revi. He hadn't had time to write a letter, but this would suffice for a goodbye. "My skewed beliefs led me to... almost make a huge mistake." She scoffed quietly. He ignored it; this was difficult enough without addressing her discontent with his word choices. "Maybe if I find the king and queen, finish restoring the Court to entirely whole, I can redeem myself—I can help the Court in a true, meaningful way."

Her eyes had softened slightly by the time he finished. "I see. Will you return, then, after that?"

He shrugged. It would be better if he didn't, probably.

"I think..." She hesitated, picking through her words. "I think Revi would want you to."

Her words stirred the hope he'd been crushing since he'd made his decision. Revi wanting him to did not mean he *should*. He'd done enough damage.

"And you?" He tossed her a light smile to hide his turmoil. "Would you appreciate my return?"

Her gaze met his, reserved but lacking the hatred he'd expected. Instead, it was full of censure, reproof. "I want Revi surrounded by good men and women who will stay loyal to him."

Enlo swallowed. "As do I." He broke eye contact, looking out the open door. Snow drifted from the sky, melding with the white that already carpeted the ground. "I'm sorry for tricking you. For everything I did in the name of the Court."

"I forgive you." The words were soft, hardly more than a whisper. She shifted closer, drawing Enlo's gaze back to her. "And I know Revi does too. Don't exile yourself forever."

Enlo stepped away, toward the threshold. He ran a hand through his hair and cast her one last lopsided smile. "I'm sure you'll see me again, Winter Princess."

A hint of a smile graced her lips. "I'll take that as a promise, for Revi's sake."

A surprised chuckle rolled from Enlo. There had been no Elyri magic lacing those words. He was not bound by them.

But maybe... maybe he would heed them anyway. Maybe one day he would return. For the Winter Court. For Revi.

Maybe. But first, he would go, to serve the Court in the best way he could right now.

CHAPTER 35
REVI

"**T**his is madness."

Revi looked up from his hands. It had been a few hours since he'd woken up—since Kienna had saved him, since Enlo had left. Revi had bathed and dressed, the motions strange and unfamiliar after so long as a beast. Then he had joined his wife—another thing to marvel over, that word—in the side room Zoya had put them in just as Kienna had almost finished telling her father all that had transpired since he had left her at the gates over a month before. Revi flexed his fingers, enjoying the feel of them as he looked at Boden.

Kienna's father sat stiffly, his hand on his sword hilt, seeming ready to leap up and drag Kienna from the room at any moment.

She seemed unflustered by his outburst. "It might be a bit mad, perhaps," she agreed lightly, "but that doesn't make it less true."

"Doesn't it?" her father asked, eyes narrowing as they flicked to Revi. "How can I know you aren't bewitched by charms or magic?"

"Papa—" Kienna began, but Revi leaned forward and met Boden's gaze.

"I swear on the life of your daughter, on the lives of my parents, and on my Court that it is all true."

"I have no proof that what the elves told me is true," Boden argued stubbornly. "I have no proof that you can't lie or trick me or my daughter in some other fashion."

Revi tipped his head in acknowledgment. "True. You cannot know that for certain. And if you do not trust your own daughter's words because you fear enchantment, then you will not trust her when she says as much, either. So, perhaps a show of good faith is in order. Give me a task, any task, and I will fulfill it to the best of my ability."

Boden's brows rose. It seemed the man was certain of his stance. He hadn't expected to get even that much from Revi. It was as if he merely waited for Revi to show his true intentions. He was going to be horribly disappointed when he realized.

It was a marvelous start to their new familial relationship.

"Anything?" Boden asked.

"Anything." He would do whatever it took to assure Boden.

"No," Kienna cut in, shaking her head violently. "No. Anything within *reason*, Papa. You may not ask him to cut off his own head or anything else equally awful."

Boden scoffed, but Revi cast Kienna a grateful glance. He did not want to impose any restrictions when the whole point was to gain her father's trust, but he appreciated her prudence in making the amendment.

Boden watched their silent exchange with a suspicious glare. "Allow my daughter to leave," he said after a moment. "Rescind the previous bargain and allow her to return home. That is my request."

"If that is what she wishes, so be it," Revi agreed, though his heart clenched in his chest. If she had been lying to him, was withholding her true feelings, this would be how he lost her.

"A marvelous idea, Papa," Kienna said. "I would like to get my own belongings and collect my rabbits." She turned to Revi with a hopeful look. "That would be all right, wouldn't it? I would love for you to meet Mushroom. And perhaps we can stay awhile so you can see where I grew up."

The vise on Revi's heart loosened. "You want me to come with you?"

She quirked an eyebrow at him. "Of course I do."

Boden protested. "*He* was never invited—"

Kienna turned back to her father with a steely look. "Whether or not you believe me, Papa, everything I've said is true. And you'll just have to find a way to accept it, because Revi and I are married—which you would know if you hadn't interrupted my tale."

"I would love to join you in Makaria," Revi added quickly. Best to get his intentions fully out into the open before Boden exploded from this latest revelation. He looked at his father-in-law again, doing his best to appear open and nonthreatening. "I would also like you to contact your queen. I think it's high time the Winter Court renewed relations with their human neighbors."

Boden's mouth dropped open even as Kienna grinned. His gaze didn't seem to know where to land. They flicked from Kienna, to Revi, to the small distance between them that his paling skin said he understood in a new light now.

"He really means it." He finally managed to find words. "All of this. It's all true."

"Yes," Revi said, even as Kienna rolled her eyes. "I am perfectly serious."

"That means… my son-in-law is a fae."

"It does mean that, doesn't it?" Kienna agreed brightly. "Holidays will be so exciting from now on."

Boden was too busy staring at Revi, taking him in with new comprehension, to respond to that tease.

"How old are you?" he finally spluttered.

Revi blinked. Of all the things the man could focus on, he chose that. What did Revi's age matter?

"A hundred and seven," he said, eliciting bulging eyes from Boden and a startled, breathy laugh from Kienna. He frowned. "I'm still quite young for an Elyri. I only reached my majority several years ago."

Boden's skin had taken on a sickly pallor.

Kienna stood. "I think we should prepare to leave. It's late, but if we make preparations tonight, we can set out first thing in the morning."

Revi rose, a small part of him enjoying the height that came with being a man instead of a beast.

"I've already told my steward to prepare rooms for you and your men," he said to Boden. "And my chefs should have supper ready by now. If there is anything you're in want of, you have only to ask. My home is your own. Now and always."

Kienna moved to her father's side and pressed a kiss to his cheek. "Good night, Papa. I'll see you in the morning."

He nodded faintly and left the room in a half daze. Revi watched him go.

"I don't think we've heard the end of his protests," he observed.

Kienna's smile curved up in a way that made Revi want to thoroughly kiss her as she watched the door her father had just left through.

"Most likely not, but he'll accept it eventually. When he realizes that I truly do love you and that you aren't as beastly as he thought."

"Most of the time," Revi corrected.

Kienna laughed. "Most of the time." She turned bright eyes toward Revi. "Do you really want to treat with Queen Riona?"

"I do," he said. "I've married a human woman. Why stop there? Perhaps if I hadn't been so tied up in my own pride regarding humans, I wouldn't have left my Court in such a sorry state for so long."

"Perhaps." She curled her fingers through his. "Personally, I'm glad it all worked out the way it did."

"As am I."

"And I'm glad," she added with a teasing smile and a glint in her eyes, "that you're open to further relations with humans."

Something about the way she said it sparked over Revi's skin. He cleared his throat. "I am."

Her smile widened, sparkling brighter than midday snow.

Oh, how he wanted to kiss her. But it all felt too fresh, too new. Too uncertain. He didn't want to take liberties and push her in ways she wouldn't be comfortable with.

At the same time, he wanted her to *know*, for there to be no room for doubt of his interest, of his devotion. He stepped closer, not quite touching her. "I am," he repeated, his eyes burning into hers. He could hear her heartbeat spike. "I am *very* interested."

Kienna bit her lip, nearly undoing his resolve to give her space and time.

"Are you hungry?" she asked.

He blinked at the abrupt subject change and leaned back. Perhaps he had pushed too much after all. "Not really. But if you are, I can..."

"I'm not," she said quickly. "And I would much prefer to spend my first married night alone with my husband"—her heartbeat increased and her cheeks tinged in a blush—"than eating with my father's soldiers."

"Would you?" He barely dared to hope in case he was misunderstanding her words.

"Yes," she whispered, stepping closer, closing the distance between them and brushing her fingers across his chest like she had once before in her dream.

A pleased growl rumbled through him, and Kienna's eyes widened before she burst into a delighted laugh.

"Most of the time, indeed." Her eyes twinkled. "Perhaps refrain from growling around my father."

He leaned into her fingers. "I'm afraid you'll have to refrain from touching me around him, then."

She bit her lip again, this time to hold back a smile.

Enough. Better to be straightforward and know where he stood with her than this half-wondering, half-hoping agony.

"Kienna, my wife." She gave a happy little hum at the title, emboldening him to continue. "This is new. I understand if you require time, so I leave it to you. Do you want me to escort you to your old room... or to ours?"

Her blush deepened at his word choice, but she barely hesitated—and it seemed more from nerves than misgivings—before she responded. "Ours, if you please."

He didn't bother trying to stop the delighted growl that rumbled through him again as he leaned in, gathering her up in his arms and kissing her.

She laughed against his lips, a sensation that he was instantly certain he wanted to experience every day for the rest of his life.

After he thoroughly kissed her, she leaned back, not pulling from his hold, just far enough so she could meet his eyes.

"I suppose I'll have to accept that you'll always be a bit feral."

He grinned wolfishly at her and pressed a kiss to her jaw.

Another breathy laugh escaped her as she craned back to look at him again. "I think it will take far longer to get used to the idea of your age. You're older than my grandfather."

Revi snorted. "Yes. Though, for an Elyri, I'm quite young. It's rare for someone my age to be handed a throne."

The thought sobered him. Kienna seemed to sense it; she pressed her hand to rest against his chest, a gentle squeeze of understanding.

Suddenly, she frowned. "Does that mean I'm to grow old while you're still in your prime?" Her eyes darted up to his. "Are you going to have to watch me die one day?"

Revi shook his head. "Our bond means we share everything. Including our lives, in the most literal sense. As long as my magic stays strong, my life—and yours—will extend far longer than a human's would." He hesitated. "Are you... comfortable with that?"

Her expression was solemn, but after a moment, she nodded. "It will be strange watching my family age without me, but..." She leaned into him, and he pressed his forehead to hers. "I chose you, not just because I wanted to save your life, but because I chose *you*. I will take everything that comes with that, good and ill."

"As will I." His grip tightened on her. "I would die for you, and I will live for you even more than for my Court." He shrugged. "Perhaps that makes me a terrible leader. Perhaps I should have let Enlo—" He cut off, his heart contracting at the thought of his cousin, leaving with only a message for him through Kienna. He closed his eyes against the wash of pain.

"You're a great leader." Kienna moved her hands to cup his face. "You've proven that plenty recently. Don't start doubting yourself again now. Besides, you'll have me to remind you."

The thought was a balm. However imperfect he was, Kienna's goodness would help him stay the course. He had no doubt that even if his people were uncertain of her at first, eventually she would become hope to them. Just like she had for him.

"I will." He opened his eyes and met her gaze. "And that reminds me. I have something for you."

Her brow knit together quizzically.

"*Zenovor.*" Magic threaded from him into her, but it took far less—or maybe he just felt the loss of it less with the curse broken—than it had to gift language to Zoya.

"Now," he whispered in Elyri, brushing his thumb across her cheek, "you are ready to be the Winter Princess our people need."

Her lips parted and eyes widened. "Did you just—" she said in Elyri, and then gasped. "I can..."

"Yes."

Her eyes narrowed. "Are you telling me that you could have gifted me with your language from the beginning instead of me trying to bumble my way through it? I made a fool of myself."

Revi grinned. "Not at all. Your determination is admirable, and your progress was impressive."

She looked pleased for half a moment before her frown returned. "Still." She whacked his arm lightly. "The whole time!"

He laughed and gathered her up again in his arms. "I'm truly sorry. Let me make it up to you."

The half-formed noise of protest died in her throat as he pressed his lips to hers.

HAPPILY EVER AFTER

With the Curse's hold on the Winter Court broken, the Winter Prince rules over his frozen lands with his beautiful bride at his side. Many wonder at his choice of bride—a human? Weak as they are?

But none of those who know the full story of the Winter Court question it, for they know their prince's true heart, and they see the beauty of their princess in her every word and deed and action.

The prince and princess are good and fair, and their happiness is almost entirely complete, if it were not for the missing piece: a cousin like a brother, the one who hasn't returned home in far too long. His presence is missed keenly, but—the whisperers say—he's on a quest to redeem himself before he can return home. Not at the prince's behest, for the prince wishes his cousin by his side as friend and counselor like in years past. No, the hunt for redemption is of the cousin's own doing. Some say he's hunting down every last monster so they will no longer haunt the Winter Court. Others say he searches for the missing Queen and King. Only the prince and princess truly know, but even they wonder, for no one has seen him since he left the Winter Court.

Even so, the prince and princess are deeply in love, and their care for each other and their people has led the Winter Court to thrive. The ones who know them say they will almost certainly live happily ever after.

Next in the Once Upon A Prince series

Check out the first book in the *Once Upon A Prince* series:

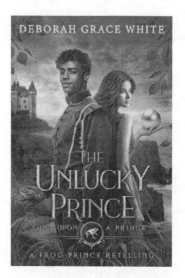

Available now!

A sacrifice to duty. Magic gone awry. And a prince with the worst luck on the continent.

Prince Ari has always struggled to find his place in his own king-dom...maybe because he spent half his childhood trapped in a swan's body. His mother thinks he should find a wife and settle down, but far from being subdued by his past brush with magic, he's convinced life has more adventure for him yet. That belief takes him to the neighbor-ing kingdom—their former enemies who are now their allies.

Princess Violet expects nothing from the foreign prince's visit, except maybe a last chance for some lighthearted fun. After all, she still has a few days before carrying out her secret plan to sacrifice her heart for the sake of the kingdom. Prince Ari will be leaving soon, so where's the harm in a bit of flirtation?

Except neither of them have any idea of the forces working against their plans, both from inside the castle and from within their own hearts. And that's before Ari falls afoul of the worst luck imaginable. As it turns out, being cursed to be a frog is even worse than being a swan.

Ari's apparent absence only clears the way for darker plots, but fortu-nately amphibians see things humans don't. It will take both a deter-mined princess and a more-than-usually resourceful frog to uncover what's really going on before it's too late—both for Violet's heart and the future of the kingdom.

The Unlucky Prince, a retelling of The Frog Prince, is book 1 of *Once Upon A Prince*, a multi-author series of clean fairy tale retellings. Each standalone novella features a swoony prince and his flaws, growth, and happily ever after.

Read The Unlucky Prince today!

ONCE UPON A PRINCE SERIES LIST

Once Upon A Prince

The Unlucky Prince by Deborah Grace White

The Beggar Prince by Kate Stradling

The Golden Prince by Alice Ivinya

The Wicked Prince by Celeste Baxendell

The Midnight Prince by Angie Grigaliunas

The Poisoned Prince by Kristin J. Dawson

The Silver Prince by Lyndsey Hall

The Shoeless Prince by Jacque Stevens

The Silent Prince by C. J. Brightley

The Crownless Prince by Selina R. Gonzalez

The Awakened Prince Alora Carter

The Winter Prince by Constance Lopez

Grab the whole Once Upon A Prince series today!

AFTERWORD

Thanks for reading The Winter Prince!

If you enjoyed the story, please consider leaving a review on Amazon or Goodreads. In doing so, you'll be helping your fellow readers find the perfect next book for them! And I will be eternally grateful for every single review I receive.

If you're interested in reading more stories from Kasmia, you have options!

If you want to read *Of Fae and Fiends* (or any of my other free short stories), a bonus scene about Revi and Kienna going to meet with Queen Riona and King Tristan, sign up for my newsletter! I email every other week with new releases, deals, and bookish ramblings.

Sign up at: https://www.constancelopez.com/newsletter

To read about Riona and how she planned to kill the crown prince to regain her throne, get *Of Stormlarks and Silence* on Amazon.

To kill the prince, she must first kill her heart.

Princess Riona was eight when the Revonian king murdered her family and conquered her kingdom with a mysterious magic. She has spent the last decade training—and waiting for her moment to avenge them all and reclaim her rightful title.

Now that the king is ailing, Riona secures a position within the Revonian royal palace. Her goals? Get close to the prince. Kill him. Uncover Revon's secret magic. Make the king suffer. Only then can she take back her country.

But the closer she gets to the prince, the more he surprises her with kindness, honor, and wit. He is nothing like his cruel father. Worse yet, he sees right through to her heart. When she planned this assassination, her heart didn't factor in.

And now it's about to ruin all her plans.

Perfect for fans of Tara Grayce, Shari Tapscott, and Kenley Davidson, *Of Stormlarks and Silence* is a slow-burn clean YA romantic fantasy standalone in the Kasmian Chronicles, a series of romantic fantasy connected standalones.

Find *Of Stormlarks and Silence* at: https://www.amazon.com/dp/ B0B7CMCBWY

You can learn more about me, my books, and the world of Kasmia at

www.constancelopez.com

Acknowledgments

Thank you to each and every reader. You are why I write, and I hope this book brought a little more joy and light into your life while you were reading it.

Thank you to every single one of the UOAP authors: Deborah, Kate, Alice, Celeste, Angie, Kristin, Lyndsey, Jacque, CJ, Selina, and Alora. I loved working with y'all on this series, and getting to know you better. You are all talented, funny, brilliant ladies. Thanks for giving this crazy idea a chance!

Thank you, once again, to Belle, for wading through the MESSIEST version of this story and making my life infinitely easier in the process. You are priceless.

Thank you to my alpha readers, Janice, Karyne, Jessica, Jacque, and Kate for reading the first version, talking through it all with me, and putting up with (and helping me tone down) axe murderer creepy psycho Enlo. You made the story so much stronger, as always! And thank you to my beta readers, Jessica, Celeste, Lindsay, Meagan, and Selina, for helping me fine-tune the characters and their arcs even more. You are each and every one of you wonderful and I'm glad you're in my life.

Thank you to Laura. You always do such an incredible job on the editing—it's a joy going through your comments, which is the best way to finish up a book.

Thank you, Gerry, for your insight, support, and hugs. I love you.

ABOUT THE AUTHOR

Constance Lopez knows magic is real. Dragons, faeries... and don't even get her started on unicorns. She grew up having epic duels in the woods with her siblings, and nature is still one of her favorite places to be. If she isn't out there thinking about her stories, she's dragging her children and husband on adventures (they always enjoy it once they're outside). Except in summer. For those months she hides inside, because Texas heat is real and it hates her.

Books have always been her haven and inspiration, and now she writes her own noblebright and romantic stories, hoping to pass those feelings along to others. Fantasy, of course. Because everything is better with magic.

To learn more, follow her on social media, or contact her:

Website: www.constancelopez.com
Facebook: https://www.facebook.com/constancelopezauthor/
Instagram: https://www.instagram.com/constancelopezauthor/
Amazon Author Page: https://www.amazon.com/Constance-Lopez/e/B09W4WQGTR

Made in the USA
Middletown, DE
21 December 2023

46670709R00128